THE WANDERER

THE WANDERER

Régine Robin

with a new afterword by the author

Translated by
Phyllis Aronoff

Alter Ego Editions
Montreal

Alter Ego Editions
3447 Hôtel-de-Ville Avenue
Montreal, Quebec H2X 3B5
Canada

First published as *La Québécoite* by Québec/Amérique in 1983
© XYZ éditeur and Régine Robin 1983, 1993

Cover artwork: Daniela Zekina
Cover and text design: Jonathan Paterson
Printed by Marc Veilleux Imprimeur Inc.

Canadian Cataloguing in Publication Data

Robin, Régine
[Québécoite. English]
The wanderer

Translation of: La Québécoite.
ISBN 1-896743-00-5

I. Aronoff, Phyllis II. Title. III. Title:
Québécoite. English.

PS8585.O335Q4213 1997   C843'54   C97-900544-2
PQ3919.2.R63Q4213 1997

Legal deposit, Bibliothèque nationale du Québec and
the National Library of Canada, 2nd quarter 1997.

To my students at the Université du Québec à Montréal, the Université de Montréal, McGill University, Université Laval, and the Université de Sherbrooke, 1974–1981.

Translator's Preface

How do you translate a book that's not in *one* language, that teems with voices from within and between different languages? A book that flouts linguistic conventions, flirts with a variety of linguistic and cultural codes, flaunts its refusal to be tied down by any one code. This is the challenge I faced when I decided to translate Régine Robin's *La Québécoite*. How to convey to the English-speaking reader the rich multiplicity of languages and voices in this book.

There is the Parisian French of the unnamed wanderer, in many variations, from chatter overheard in cafés to erudite references to the songs and slogans of left-wing culture. There is the French of Quebec in its many variations, an unexpectedly foreign language, "neither the same nor other." And since this is Montreal, there is English, a constant unsettling yet enriching presence. There is also Yiddish, a subtext that occasionally surfaces, representing the idealized world of the *shtetl* now irretrievably lost. All these languages co-exist in dialogue, confrontation, cacophony—and, it would seem, mutual untranslatability. One of the questions posed by *The Wanderer* is precisely whether translation is possible at all, given the heavy burden of history and collective memory that every language carries.

The wanderer seeks not only a voice in Quebec, a common language in which to make herself heard here, but also something much more fundamental, an anchor, a fixed point of reference, to give her world shape, consistency, density. For Régine Robin—as for the Kabbalists who constitute yet another voice in this book —language is not only a means of communication; it has the power to bring the world into being. Words, stories, narrative create the world and the self, making, unmaking, and remaking identity.

But at the same time, "every story hides a corpse." Every neat, seamless narrative with a beginning-middle-end, a single voice, is achieved at the expense of silencing other voices (the book's original title, a wonderfully pointed play on words, means, roughly, "the silent Quebecker," the voice *not* heard in Quebec). For Robin, it is an ethical imperative—and not merely an aesthetic choice—to preserve the many voices, to refuse to let them be drowned out by one voice or subsumed within a single story. Thus her use of a many-voiced narrative form.

As translator of this book, I had to make its ethical imperative my own. As much as possible, I wanted to have English-speaking readers share—as the readers of the original do—the heroine's experience of the voices within and around her, especially the mix of French and English that is part of life in Montreal. One consequence is that *The Wanderer* contains a surprising amount of French for a book translated *from* French. Readers who live in that city may find nothing strange about this: they are to some extent already living between languages.

Perhaps we all live between languages much more than is normally acknowledged. We all confront and contain multitudes of voices. And we all negotiate our way through and across these differences by means of a constant process of translation. Those of us who call ourselves translators are just more conscious of the process. As a translator, then, I can hardly do otherwise than believe that languages, voices, stories, histories *are* translatable, at least in principle, even though in practice I am acutely aware of what gets lost in translation.

I

Snowdon

. . . this is why I dreamed of a work which would not enter into any category, fit any genre, but contain them all; a work hard to define, but defining itself precisely by this lack of definition; a work which would not answer to any name, but had donned them all; a work belonging to no party or persuasion; a work of earth in the sky and of sky on earth; a work which would be the rallying point of all the words scattered in space whose loneliness and discomfiture we do not suspect; the place beyond all place of an obsession with God, unquenched desire of a mad desire; a book, finally, which would only surrender by fragments, each of them the beginning of another book.

—Edmond Jabès, *Aely, The Book of Questions*

They existed among three impossibilities, which I just happen to call linguistic impossibilities. It is simplest to call them that. But they might also be called something entirely different. These are: The impossibility of not writing, the impossibility of writing German, the impossibility of writing differently. One might also add a fourth impossibility, the impossibility of writing (since the despair could not be assuaged by writing, was hostile to both life and writing; writing is only an expedient, as for someone who is writing his will shortly before he hangs himself—an expedient that may well last a whole life). Thus what resulted was a literature impossible in all respects, a gypsy literature which had stolen the German child out of its cradle and in great haste put it through some kind of training, for someone has to dance on the tightrope. (But it wasn't even a German child, it was nothing; people merely said that somebody was dancing).

—Franz Kafka, letter to Max Brod, 1921

N o ORDER. No chronology, no logic, no lodging. Nothing but a desire for writing and this proliferation of existence. To fix this porousness of the probable, this micro-memory of strangeness. To spread out all the signs of difference: bubbles of memories, pieces of vague reminiscences coming all together without texture, a bit grey. Without order, they were loose series, colours without contours, lights without brightness, lines without objects. Fleeting. The black night of exile. History in pieces. To fix this strangeness before it became familiar, before the wind suddenly changed, freeing rushes of obvious images. The longings could be experienced but they couldn't be tamed. You couldn't analyze them. They would suddenly impose themselves. No representation of exile. Unrepresentable. With no present, no past. Just blurry faraways, bits, traces, fragments, gazes all along these urban travellings. To fix the strangeness right away because the longing would break through the surface of the days by surprise. It was language, language taking its pleasure all alone, body without subject. Nothing but language. It was snatches at first, of conversations heard in cafés, along the streets, in lines waiting, in the métro. It's a settlement. You're not trying to understand. It has nothing to do with a contract. Look, I'll tell you something. I'm selling the building on Rue Censier to the common property. I don't know. The contributions aren't equal, ninny. Separate as to property? You don't think about it. It's true, listen, it's logical. With the inheritance from my parents, I buy another building— incidentally, you know, it's proportional to our contributions, but no, you have to make a big thing out of it. You're beautiful, beautiful, don't ever use makeup again. You understand, it couldn't go on. I told him. Snatches whispered in the dark at the movies. It's a building on Avenue Foch. If I get kicked out, what will you do? That slut Nicole. And what if I had nothing, if I didn't have anything. If you find someone better than me, you leave, and all I have is myself. That's the problem. You're an idiot. Half-whispered snatches, confusion. Confessions. Misunderstandings. That's not what I meant. What I mean is. You said it. You didn't say it, say it, tell me, repeat, don't say that. A building on Avenue Foch, did you say? He owed money. Let's go, let's leave. It's not very nice out, not warm. Already summer, but we won't have any summer this year. It upsets me, I'm already all jittery. Let the sky fall on my head. Horn, brakes, squeal of brakes in the rain, spraying, splashing. They're in no hurry to serve us. She'll make an omelette. We'll see. A Ricard and a Casanis, please. Sounds of pinball machines, of cassettes playing low or spewing noise. But still, there aren't fifty million morons. I'll remember later. He had a problem yesterday, work bothered him—I don't know anything about it. Of course not. What does that mean? We don't know anything about it. What do you feel like eating? Green and red stripes from the traffic lights at the corner, greenish reflections of the crosses of pharmacies, dazzling, headlights flashing. The voices move away, move closer. Their inflections are unpredictable. Every year he says he'll retire. If only he didn't bother people with it. The Pernod is sweet—it tastes different. What a nut! Cheap bracelets at Félix Potin. A decaf please. Sounds of buses, of the cash register. Hoarse voices, warm voices, mingling of voices. I touch them, I finger them, I hug them to me. Bits of dreary everyday, snatches of radio broadcasts, television theme songs. Zitrone. Giquel. El Kabbach. Hit parade, ads, news, TV newsmagazine. Scraps of routes along the métro lines. Line 10. Austerlitz without sun, without victory. We were leaving for the Landes. The smell of urine and vomit always dominated the station. Sadness, dirt, the station crossed, the endless wait for a taxi on the return, the arrival early in the morning, the first *café crème* after vacation. You had arranged to meet your husband in Rouyn-Noranda, at the local bistrot on a little square—but there was no square and no local bistrot in Noranda-Rouyn. The meeting with a city. You often got lost, coming back to the same place a thousand times, recognizing the signs, the shops, the quality of the air hanging over the intersections. A month later, familiar routes had replaced the hesitant, awkward wanderings of the early days. Cities take on colour in the early morning. There are also colourless cities tinted with water, snow. Fog and siren cities, factory smokestack cities, park cities, flower cities. You loved all cities. The hallucinatory breathing of American cities seen from a plane at night, like an instrument panel, an electronic screen of criss-crossed lines of light, webs of light in the night.

Downtown,
old ring,
new ring,
outer boulevards,
beltways,
boulevards periphériques,
ramps,
highways,
freeways,
turnpikes,
parkways,
thruways,
Stadmitte,
Zentrum,
midtown,
downtown,
centreville.

This desire for writing. Yet it was so simple to start at the beginning, to follow a plot, to resolve it, to speak of an off-place, a non-place, an absence of place. To try to fix a few signs, hold onto them, wrest them from the void. Nothing but a mark, a tiny little mark. You had to fix all the signs of difference: the difference of the smells, of the colour of the sky, the difference of the landscape. You had to make an inventory, a catalogue, a nomenclature. To record everything in order to give more body to this existence. Your slightest doings, your encounters, your appointments, your movements—the curious names of the big stores:

SIMPSON
EATON
THE BAY
OGILVY
HOLT RENFREW
MARKS & SPENCER
WOOLWORTH
KRESGE
DOMINION
STEINBERG

All this would surely end up having the density of a life, an everyday life. Would it be possible to find a position in language, a purchase, a fixed point of reference, a stable point, something that would anchor the words when there was only a tremulous trace of text, a mute voice, twisted words? To take the right to speak. What words? To keep quiet? Humiliation again? To wear the star again? Broken text. To root out fear, shame, solitude. To speak for—for nothing perhaps. To speak because. The noise— nothing but noise, babble, rubble.

> I don't know how to speak, exclaims Moses
> perhaps to keep quiet—
> but a voice, a little tinkling voice
> to cross the violent sheets of silence—

just speech—words to the letter
it's the unfinished that's important—
　　death
　　is but a shadow
There will be no beginning
　　no story
No order—no chronology
　　no logic
　　no lodging—
omega will never come. Because nothing starts at
alpha—the first letter of the Bible is *bet,* the second
letter; the last letter is *tav,* index of the future
　　open—
to keep quiet perhaps—
　　perhaps—
To write—with the six million letters of the Jewish
alphabet

You had loved this country, you had breathed in the blue
mist, the autumnal smells of fresh-baked bread and dead leaves,
the currents of cool air on the milky mountain. JUSSIEU. The
polonia trees in the square, the newspaper kiosque and the student cafés across from the university. CARDINAL LEMOINE.
Going up the street to get to the Mouffe. King Henry at the corner of Rue des Boulangers, where we bought Glenfiddich and
Pilsener beer. Continuing on Rue Monge to the square—bistrots,
market twice a week, the shade of chestnut trees, evening on
Place Monge. MAUBERT-MUTUALITÉ. How many meetings
at La Mutualité, the hall empty or full? Everyone to La Mutu! We
aren't going to La Mutu! On October 27, 1960, we didn't go to
La Mutu—who remembers? How many Algerian wars, strikes,
frustrations, celebrations, rages, commemorations at La Mutu?
MABILLON. The student restaurant before the Mazet opened.
We went to the Mab, it was better than the Inter. SÈVRES-

BABYLONE. The Bon Marché store and the Lutétia café. It was before they built the Maison des Sciences de l'Homme. Already the nice neighbourhoods. VANNEAU. Chez Germaine, on Rue Pierre-Leroux. A greasy spoon where everyone knew each other, where the owner went around with a tea towel. When you wanted to wipe your hands, you'd yell, "Germaine, the towel!" Germaine's Basque chicken and cherry clafoutis. Café Vanneau right near the métro, where you could read on the walls about the bird the place was named for:

> The lapwing is found in Kamchatka and Europe, where its habits and migrations are similar. It has very strong wings and uses them a great deal. It flies for long periods at a time, rising very high. On the ground, it darts, jumps, and moves in short flights. This bird is very cheery and is always in sprightly movement, frolicking in the air. It holds itself for several seconds in all kinds of positions, even with its breast upward or on its side with its wings perpendicular, and no bird gambols and flutters about more nimbly.
>
> [signed] BUFFON

Conversations barely intercepted. I'll call you. I'll give you a ring. Don't go. Give me a ring. Call me. I love you. I don't love you. Tell me you love me. Of course I love you. I love you with cream, I don't love you with chocolate. Regret for words already spoken, crystallized, stored up, itemized. DUROC. Café François-Coppée and Boulevard du Montparnasse. The imagination of a distant city. False returns. Her name is despair. As usual, right. I don't know why I have this tune in my head—la la la la. Don't be mad at me, my little Loulou, if the cops are on my tail. The imagination clings to puddles, gutters, sidewalks. It was a pale grey menu, a bistrot menu. They tumbled out in purple memory layers. All the cafés with their different names. There were the Bougnats

Bougnat des Folies
Bougnat de Lagny
the Chopes

10

Chope de Choisy
Chope de Montreuil
Chope lorraine
Chope des martyrs
Chope des sports
Chope normande
just La Chope
  on the Place de la
  CONTRESCARPE
 There were the CANONS
   CANON de TOLBIAC
  and
   the BOUQUETS
   BOUQUET DE VERSAILLES
   BOUQUET DE L'OPÉRA
   BOUQUET DU NORD
   BOUQUET DE BELLEVILLE
   BOUQUET D'ALÉSIA
 There were the CARREFOURS
   THE TERMINUSES
   THE BARS DE LA POSTE
      DE LA PAIX
      DES SPORTS
   THE CLAIRONS
   THE MARRONIERS
   THE TROUBADOURS
   THE SAUVIGNONS
   not counting THE DUPONTS
  NO JEWS OR DOGS ALLOWED
   DURING THE WAR.

Like the failure of exile itself. It's all one or all the other.
How much did you say? They're going to pay you? Before the
end of the year? A good strong espresso. Good. I'm getting out.

I'm shoving off. I'm taking off. I'm hitting the road. I'm off. I'm weighing anchor. I'm setting sail. Sailing. "After sailing for three months, they arrived. It was a dangerous crossing. The ship pitched and rolled, even in good weather. The round-keeled sailboats were unstable. 'You will pay 6000 pounds,' states the royal order of March 12, 1534, 'to the navigator Jacques Cartier, who is going to the New Founde Landes to discover certain islands and countries where large amounts of gold are said to be found.'"

Hello, asthmatic breathing of the city. You're feeling good. The pink neighbourhoods, the lilac neighbourhoods, the blue neighbourhoods, the grey neighbourhoods. Wanderings. Strolls. Listening to the sounds, the smells—cinnamon cities, curry cities, onion cities.

    Stops at storefronts
    crossings in covered passageways
    return to the large squares
    descents into train stations.

To feel the wind, the fine rain, the murky reflections in the puddles. What anguish some evenings with the sidewalks eternally wet. To fix the difference of all these banks scattered through the city like flies:

    Canadian National Bank
    Canadian Imperial Bank of Commerce
    Bank of Montreal
    Bank of Nova Scotia
    Savings Bank
    Bank of Canada
    Federal Development Bank
    Mercantile Bank of Canada
    Provincial Bank of Canada
    Toronto Dominion Bank

bank—bank—the land of banks—the big bank country—the big bank power
    in God we bank

She would live in Snowdon, west of the mountain and the Notre-Dame-des-Neiges cemetery, on one of the shady streets around Victoria, parallel or perpendicular to Queen Mary. A neighbourhood of immigrants with awkward English, where the accents of central Europe still survive, where you hear Yiddish spoken and it's easy to find pickles, braided challah, matzoh meal.

They would live in the ramshackle house of an old aunt who had come here just before the war, by chance probably, like Mordecai Richler's grandparents. The grandfather had sailed to Canada third class, leaving a *shtetl* in Galicia in 1904 right after the start of the Russo-Japanese War and the horrible pogrom at Kishinev. He originally had a railway ticket to Chicago. On the boat, he met another Jew from the same sect who had family in Chicago and a ticket for Montreal. The grandfather knew someone who had a cousin in Toronto, which he discovered was in Canada. One morning on the deck, the two men exchanged their tickets.

But no. That's not how Mime Yente would have come. She would have left her native Volhynia in March 1919, when the soldiers of Petlyura, having beaten the Red Army, took Zhitomir. Her father, the baker in the market square, would have been killed by the Whites—found strangled amid his round loaves, with his eyes wide open. In London, Mime Yente would have married Moishe. They would have settled in the East End, in Whitechapel, finding work in a clothing factory, a sweatshop. More than once in those terrible years, they would have been seen at the soup kitchen on Brune Street, as poor as Job. Moishe would have worked tirelessly in the Jewish trade union movement, in the radical scene that was then seething with activity. They would have been through the general strike of 1926, which lasted nine days. The aunt would still remember speaking to the troops that occupied the neighbourhood. Then, with the money they had saved by working like slaves, with incredible determination, they would have bought a bakery, a *bakerai,* on Fashion Street in the heart of the old ghetto. A miserable storefront, but no matter! They would have become real celebrities, suppliers to Bloom's, the famous restaurant where all the Jews from central Europe went. Yente would still be able to tell stories about Jack the Ripper and Martha Turner, Polly Nichols, Annie Chapman, Elizabeth Stride, Catherine Eddowes, and Mary Jane Kelly, his victims. The aunt would have travelled to Paris during the trial of Samuel Schwartzbard, who had killed Petlyura. Schwartzbard was a poet who had taken part in the events of 1905 and organized the Jewish self-defence during the terrible pogroms. He had escaped his pursuers and lived underground in Paris as a watchmaker. Back in Russia in 1917, he had rejoined the Red Army. Then, in 1920, much of his family had been slaughtered by Petlyura's troops. After that, his one goal had been to find Petlyura and kill him—which he did in May 1926. The aunt would have been a witness at his trial.

"The man was a liberator. He avenged us. He gave us back our dignity," she would have said in court, this shy little bit of a woman. Back in London, hearing of Schwartzbard's acquittal, she would have given out round loaves and challah to everyone in Whitechapel and Stepney. And then, on October 4, 1936, the aunt would have taken part in the battle of Cable Street, which pitted trade unionists, Communists, and workers against Mosley's fascists. Mosley had announced that he was organizing a march through the East End. This was immediately understood by the people in the shops as a provocation. Three thousand Blackshirts mobilized on Cable Street. At the intersection of Cable and Leman Streets, they came up against barricades erected by the crowd. More than a hundred thousand workers had massed to block their way. They shall not pass. *No pasarán.* When a truck was overturned, the police charged. Stones and bricks rained down on the cops. All the dockers from Wapping and St. George's were there. The Commissioner of Police, after arresting several workers—one must do what one must do—ordered Mosley and his troops to turn around and go back along the Embankment, where they dispersed. That night there was dancing in the East End all night long. And among the dancers was Mime Yente, with her rolls.

They would have left London just before the war, a little tired. Like so many others, Moishe and Yente would have crossed the ocean and ended up here in Snowdon. They'd have bought that ramshackle house and the tiny bakery on Décarie just north of Isabella. Almost all the customers would have been Yiddish-speaking. What a pleasure to make challah, wheat bread, balls of rye bread, and black bread with kimmel, sesame, or sunflower seeds, and bagels, little cheesecakes, strudel, and hamantashen. People would have come from all over.

Moishe would have died a long time ago. The aunt would have sold the bakery to some Hungarian Jews from Budapest. She would have retired to her house—that's where she would have greeted her—I'm not sure when. That rickety house that was sinking into ruin would be her place, her real country. A large maple tree on the street side would almost completely hide the dark, cracked brick. They would have had the lower floor of the duplex with separate entrances, while old Yente reigned imperiously over the upper. It would have been very easy for them to furnish their four rooms and basement. They would have put some old pine chests in the living room that looked out directly onto the street, with an old sofa in earth tones under the window where in the summer the leafy shadows of the maple tree played. There would be old-fashioned lace curtains from Chez Quentin and pots of plants hanging in front of the window. An oak table bought at a secondhand store on St-Denis or Duluth would go in the dining room. The two other rooms would consist of a rather monastic bedroom and a messy book-filled office with simple bricks-and-boards shelves and rough trestle tables covered with old reels of tape, multi-coloured file folders, books, pencils,

15

ashtrays, unused chequebooks, and cleared Visa and Bell bills. The basement, down a steep flight of stairs, would contain a large kitchen, the bathroom, the furnace, and a laundry room Yente would also have access to. The kitchen would be brightened by small windows that let in the daylight, at least in summer—in winter the windows would be blocked by the heavy snow. Although the kitchen was large, they wouldn't have enough money to furnish it properly. She would have dreamed of tiles on the floor and rustic pine furniture, with ivy trailing down from the top of the cupboards. They would have had to make do with a formica table—a house-warming gift from the aunt, who meant well—chairs found at a garage sale, and a stove and fridge bought on credit at The Bay, but she would have insisted on having the old-fashioned curtains here too, and a sophisticated art nouveau light fixture. The effect would be pleasant but nothing more. The bedroom, on the ground floor, would open directly onto a garden that was quite big for the neighbourhood, where Mime Yente would long ago have planted rose bushes. In summer, they'd take out the kitchen table and some deck chairs and at sunset they'd sit out in their oasis daydreaming. The guardian of the hearth would be Bilou, a lazy, music-loving marmalade cat a bit past his prime. He'd spend most of his time on the ledge in front of the middle window between the lace and the glass, taking in the view of the maple tree and the houses across the street, calmly waiting for them to come home, wondering where they could be—at the university, the library, the movies, with friends, at the store—gazing into the distance, happy to do nothing. A real cat's life. Near the front door would be the piano brought from Paris.

MÉTRO SÉGUR. The home of the teacher from the *conservatoire,* where the grand piano took up the whole of the oval sitting room, and just before taking the métro, the familiar ritual of your mother reminding you to cut your nails and wash your hands or people in the nice neighbourhood would say that Jews are dirty, and you obediently cut your nails, so that Ségur to you is not the countess of the pink library, née Rostopchine, but a brand of scissors. Nogent-Ségurs just as there are Rohan-Chabots, Rohan-Soubises, Rohan-Guemenées with queen's necklaces and round Breton hats. Would the past have to cloak itself, dagger itself? Torn, broken, in pieces—a datebook without dates, chronicler, memorialist, minutes, proceedings, seedings. The uniforms. The war.

She would be at her piano. She would spend hours there with Bilou settled on top on the pile of sheet music at the right of the metronome. He'd obviously like Chopin the best, purring along with every nocturne, every mazurka, but Czerny's scales would send him running. He would have a special way of requesting Chopin, squinting his eyes and stretching his neck. Then he would get back up on top of the piano on the sheet music, curl up in a ball, and purr along in time. Mime Yente would have come to the conclusion that Bilou had Polish connections, but were they Polack or Jewish connections?—was he a pogrom cat or a kosher cat?

She would also be trying to write, preferably a work of genius, a bestseller that would take them out of their poverty. She would amass notes, pages, files. That Loewy, who so strongly marked Kafka, was born in Warsaw in 1887 of a poor Chassidic family; that as a child he had been recruited into a troupe of *Purim spieler,* those traditional minstrels, half clowns, half folksingers, who told the wonderful story of Esther to the children of the *shtetl;* that he left Warsaw for Paris, where he became a labourer; that he finally joined a travelling troupe, which in 1911 performed in Prague, where he met Kafka; that he was exterminated in 1942; and that—and that. She would have a passion for Yiddish theatre, and dream of putting on plays by Goldfaden, returning to the tradition of Michoels—or of doing an American adaptation of the old folklore, renewing it, recreating it, a kind of tragicomic musical comedy with something like the chorus in a

Greek tragedy, which would be the voice of the murdered people, which would come in from time to time to judge or possibly change what was being said, using parody, song, and epic. She would have wanted to do Sholem Asch's *Sabbatai Sevi*, so fascinated was she by this character.

They would love the neighbourhood. Nearby, on Queen Mary, all the stores, the activity, the lights. Steinberg, Carmel Fruits and Vegetables, the Book Centre at Westbury, and further, on Décarie, the Snowdon Delicatessen, where they would go for brunch on Sunday morning around eleven-thirty or twelve. They would have bagels—Mime Yente could pick the best ones by feel—with Philadelphia cream cheese and lox or whitefish, and coffee. Mime Yente would leave after an hour but they would stay longer. They would return home later with the big Sunday *New York Times* and the *New York Review of Books*. Sometimes, instead of the delicatessen, they would go to Murray's on the other side of Décarie and watch the elderly ladies in their British-style hats. They would spend the afternoon in bed reading the big newspaper from beginning to end, making love, listening to Mozart's *Requiem* or Handel's *Messiah*, with Bilou a voyeur on the edge of the bed. They would learn in the *New York Times Book Review* that Philip Roth had become a millionaire from his *Portnoy* and that he had fled New York and was now living in some kind of manor in Connecticut—all the more reason to keep working on the future bestseller. There would also be Pumpernik's restaurant on the corner of Queen Mary and Décarie—pickles, herring, kreplach, knaidlach, gefilte fish, and especially cheesecake—

We'd be all right
right at home?
far from the tamed discourses
the trace
cut-off

what we would not find at the end of the waiting
          Off-place
          cut-off page
Here   everywhere   Elsewhere
No story   will take place   She's going
She doesn't know where.   with no markers
                with no shelters
She says nothing
She says the nothing
        in suspense
        separated from herself.
The connections are screwed up
There will be no story.
There will be no Messiah.
What we would not find at the end of the
Waiting.
Night—frost—silence
the unfinished book—the words undone.
        the words   nomadic   mad
        made in Pitchipoi

She would give a few courses in Jewish Studies at McGill
in her awkward English, having found nothing in the French
universities. An irregular, precarious job at starvation wages.
Courses on Soviet Jewish literature between the wars. She would
have spent a long time discussing this page from Isaac Babel:

> The cemetery of a little Jewish town. Assyria and all the mys-
> terious stagnation of the East, over those weedgrown plains of
> Volhynia.
>
> Carved grey stones with inscriptions three centuries
> old. Crude high-reliefs hewn out in the granite. Lambs and
> fishes depicted above a skull, and Rabbis in fur caps—Rabbis
> girt round their narrow loins with leather belts. Below their
> eyeless faces the rippling stone line of their curly beards. To

19

one side, beneath a lightning-shattered oak, stands the burial vault of the Rabbi Azrael, slain by the Cossacks of Bogdan Chmielnicki. Four generations lie buried in that vault that is as lowly as a water-carrier's dwelling; and the memorial stone, all overgrown with green, sings of them with the eloquence of a Bedouin's prayer.

"Azrael son of Ananias, Jehovah's mouthpiece.

"Elijah son of Azrael, brain that struggled single-handed with oblivion.

"Wolff son of Elijah, prince robbed from the Torah in his nineteenth spring.

"Judah son of Wolff, Rabbi of Cracow and Prague.

"O death, O covetous one, O greedy thief, why couldst thou not have spared us, just for once?'"

She would have seen in a book one day that in Wegrow, a little town east of Warsaw, the old cemetery had been turned into a football field. The cemetery of a little Jewish town. That too would henceforth belong to legend, to a mute saga she would carry inside herself, impossible to communicate.

Her husband, who would have studied at McGill and Columbia, would teach political economy at Concordia. She would have met him in New York with his jeans and guitar in Washington Square in the midst of the surprised squirrels, with the skyscrapers in the distance half swallowed up in fog. They would have spent most of the night walking around the Village. She would have taken him for a New Yorker, a bit of a hippie, with no money. His history would be rather unusual. His parents would have come to New York at the end of the war when he was a little boy. His mother being a Polish Jew, they would have been turned away on arrival because the Cold War was beginning. Without a cent, unable even to take a freighter back, they would have washed up—and that's really the word for it—in Montreal while waiting. Then when he reached school age, his father, an old partisan of secular education, would have become aware of the horrible situation. Going to enrol his son in school, he would have seen nothing but nuns and crucifixes everywhere. Idly leafing through a children's reader, he would have read:

Conjugation

Conjugate out loud in the present tense:
— To sympathize with the suffering father
— To pity his great pain
— To pray on this friendly grave
— To have death in the soul
— To weaken very quickly
— To praise the virtues of the departed one
Conjugate out loud in the present tense in the negative:
— To languish on a bed of pain
— To be on the threshold of eternity
— To forget dead relatives
— To lay a wreath
— To suffer a great loss
Put in the singular, in the negative:
— Sufferings purify the soul
— These bereavements are very recent
— We forget the dead
— These pains are healing
— The dying take communion
— These chants soften the heart

He would have opened an arithmetic book and discovered the following page:

Pilgrimage to the Oratory

Carry out the calculation to get the answer.
1. I paid 15 cents for 3 St. Joseph's medals. How much does one medal cost?
2. Two holy pictures cost 14 cents. How much does one picture cost?
3. Three rosaries cost 69 cents. How much does one rosary cost?

4. I also bought 3 cases for the rosaries. I paid 36 cents. How much does one case cost?
5. I pay 68 cents for two statues. How much does one statue cost?

Not to mention the catechism and the story of the New Testament:

Did the Jews recognize J.C. as the Messiah?
Answer: No. They were waiting for a Messiah who would rule the earth, who would be a greater warrior than David and *richer* than Solomon. They refused to recognize him in the humble son of a carpenter.

He would have seen red and stormed out—and discovered a little later that the English were willing to accept the child without imposing any Protestant religiosity. The only things he could not be exempted from would be the morning salute to the Union Jack and *God Save the King*. That would have been the price to be paid. And that's why, with his Polish mother and French leftist father, he would have gone all through school in English.

A small and humble people clutching the skirts of priests who've become sole guardians of faith, knowledge, truth and the national heritage; . . . shielded from the perilous evolution of thought by well-intentioned but misguided educators who distorted the great facts of history whenever they found it impractical to keep them totally ignorant.

He would have rejected the *grande noirceur*—and the ignorance and the priests.

In New York, he would have been sitting on a bench in Washington Square. She would have come and sat down beside him, just like that, without thinking. He would have been holding a book by Ginsberg. They would have started by exchanging banalities but would quickly have gotten past the small talk.

"I really like New York. I come here often. I did my PhD at Columbia," he would have said, lighting one cigarette from another, automatically. "I love this ocean of a city, where everyone feels at home and nowhere at the same time—it's like a huge no-man's-land, a camp of exiles, displaced persons. All of us here are halfbreeds, wild seeds—I like that."

She would have smiled a silly smile without saying anything. He would have told her the story of his life, his turbulent past. His French would be impeccable, with just a touch of an American accent. They would have left Washington Square and gone into the Village. They would have begun to feel at ease in the warmth of communication.

"What exactly do you feel you are—American, Canadian, Québécois, Jewish, French? You have a pretty complicated history."

"Yes indeed," he would have answered with a straight face, like Woody Allen. "No, it's not that complicated.
I feel like
    a New Yorker from Paris or
    a Montrealer from the *shtetl,* if you prefer."

They would have laughed, suddenly realized it was time to eat, and found a Middle Eastern restaurant on Bleeker Street. And between the feta and the baklava, they would have decided never to part. They'd love all kinds of American stuff, Walter Cronkite, Johnny Carson, Coca-Cola, Archie Bunker, and Mary Tyler Moore, not to mention *Saturday Night Live*—because they would have cable and in addition to the four Canadian networks and Radio-Québec they would be able to watch almost all the American channels. And they would talk about the Paris of the Americans, which would help when she was suddenly overcome with homesickness and longing. The American Express on Rue Scribe. What's the dollar worth? It's worth shit. And the Canadian dollar? Even less. Shakespeare and Company beside La Bûcherie near Saint-Julien-le-Pauvre church. The *Herald Tribune* seller on the Boul' Mich at the corner of Rue Monsieur-le-Prince. Big Macs at McDonald's. A joint bought for a small fortune in the crowd on Saint-Séverin. We'd make plans for the summer. Paris would have changed further, a bank in place of the bistrot remembered in a tremulous voice, the métro orange card even more expensive, the shopkeepers even more belligerent, the parking even harder, the elevated métro now silent and the lines extended to Saint-Denis and Aubervilliers, meeting the express line at Châtelet. We'd feel at home. Every once in a while, something would grate. It would come by surprise, slipping between the stitches of a tightly knit happiness. These moments of heaviness could never be predicted.

    Isolation   Being cut off?
An emptiness of something?
    Something else?
WE WOULD NEVER BECOME   TRULY
        QUÉBÉCOIS.
On the other side of the linguistic barrier?
    Okay then. She would have come from Paris
      even worse
    a damn Frenchwoman.
    A Yiddishophone imagination? What a funny word!

She would have started an impossible novel on Sabbatai Sevi, the false messiah of the seventeenth century, sort of a metaphorical reflection on History. It would be about a course assigned at the last minute to an asthmatic old writer who had been interested in the character for a long time.

Ish hayabi. Once upon a time. If they think it's that simple to tell a story, to tell History. Back in fashion, they say. A course on Sabbatai Sevi! Is that all?! Never liked that brute. Thousands of books and articles. If they think I'm going to beat my brains out over it, well! I said yes without thinking. Now I'm stuck with this course for the whole second semester. Forty-five hours to talk about Sabbatai Sevi. Three hours of lecturing, discussing Jewish History in general, talking about marking, the paper to be written, exams. My death of a cold, with my health—a little bit of

Sabbatai Sevi between asthma attacks. I'm sure to miss one class, an attack when there's a snowstorm. To stay at the pine desk under the window. A good hot cup of coffee. Sunday morning, a nice cup of coffee and bread with cream cheese and smoked salmon or whitefish. Outside, the snow blocking out the horizon behind the top branches of the maple, the sky milky. The snow. The lights of the houses across the street. A good hot coffee. My desk under the window, with dozens of books all around. The old Bedford pen found in a secondhand store in New York, with the name R. Cameron engraved on it. Old Cameron must have died a long time ago. He must have been an investment dealer or stockbroker, a horrid petty-bourgeois conformist, maybe of Italian background. The look on his face if he knew that an asthmatic old Jew had inherited his junk. At my desk. The snow. All day long in my bathrobe with Sabbatai Sevi. Thirty-nine hours of classes left to go. A student strike or a really bad snowstorm— three less hours. Twelve three-hour classes on Sabbatai Sevi. If they think I'm going to let them walk all over me. Students still in first year. Know nothing about Jewish History, often speak Yiddish at home, that's all. Think that dispenses them from having to learn anything. Think I'm an old fool. Bunch of brats. I'll show them. First History, always History—rub their noses in History. Barely know Lenin came after Saint Louis. To the two of us, the Ukraine and Podolia. From the summit of my desk, several centuries of pogroms look down upon us. Central Europe in the seventeenth century: three hours. Chmielnicki's massacres: three hours, maybe even six, there were a lot of massacres. The Jewish world and its spiritual problems after the massacres: incredibly boring class, three hours, perhaps a review of the religion. Those little idiots don't even know what the Torah is, even if they eat kosher and give money to Israel. Well-off kids from Westmount or Côte-St-Luc while I, old fool, have never been able to get out of the ghetto. The snow, at my desk at the top of the house at the height of the topmost branch of the maple tree. R. Cameron, my friend, let's not get worked up. Still eight classes to fill. The waiting for the Messiah in 1666, the Jewish world in 1666: three hours. Little jaunt to the Mediterranean region, because they'll be imagining Florida. Nothing like Miami, I'll say, don't confuse Constantinople with Fort Lauderdale. Eastern, first class, or Sunflight, popcorn and coke, or Delta, champagne even in economy class. Take it easy. And more History. The Ottoman Empire, a great class, I love it. A little exhibitionism. I love the Golden Horn. Wax lyrical on setting suns, a grandiose tone. A great civilization. The smells. Finally, Sabbatai himself. Two or three exciting classes. Don't forget his whore. Indignant protests by the more religious students in the class. The old fool's an infidel, a red, everyone knows. Go on to mythology with his conversion to Islam, buffoonery in the grand Turkish style with a touch of an Eisenstein epic. Finally, it's getting interesting. They might like it. The false messiah, the recovery of control, the Sabbataian sects, with the obligatory glance at Frank a century later. Pickles and smoked meat. The course is over—have a nice holiday. I'll be able to go back to my own concerns, if I haven't croaked by then. The snow. Sabbatai. The snow. A two-room apartment, I think. I don't see a kitchen. Just a little two-room with the stove in the middle. The cat is purring. It's snowing. I'm coming home from *cheder* with my nose running. My old galoshes leak. My coat doesn't keep me very warm. It's snowing big flakes. I'm coming back from violin lesson, not *cheder.* How much snow has since fallen, covering the old Jewish cemeteries to the tops of the gravestones. That's it—I went to play with Yankel and Chaim instead of going to violin class as usual. Memory—literature—intertext. That's what you say. It's Babel. But we had the same childhood. Except for Odessa—all I know of it is the steps in *The Battleship Potemkin,* like everyone else. No, for me it's Vitebsk, on account of Chagall. Just as well let him speak, unless it's he speaking in me, or both of us being spoken by the same childhood.

My town sad and gay!

As a boy, I used to watch you from our doorstep, childishly. To a child's eyes you were clear. When the walls cut off my view, I climbed up on a little post. If then I still could not see you, I climbed up on the roof. Why not? My grandfather used to climb up there too.

And I gazed at you as much as I pleased.

Here, in Pokrowskaja Street, I was born a second time. . . .

I roamed about the streets, I searched and prayed:

"God, Thou who hidest in the clouds or behind the shoemaker's house, grant that my soul may be revealed, the sorrowful soul of a stammering boy. Show me my way. I do not want to be like all the others; I want to see a new world."

As if in reply, the town seems to snap apart, like the strings of a violin, and all the inhabitants, leaving their usual places, begin to walk above the earth. People I know well settle down on roofs and rest there.

All the colours turn upside down, dissolve into wine, and my canvases gush it forth. . . .

Vitebsk, I'm deserting you.

Stay alone with your herring!

At least don't start out by putting them off. They'll end up firing me. A small pension, peanuts. Sent to the other world, the asthmatic quickly done in. Gone to join Sabbatai Sevi in Constantinople in a DC-10. Keep the customers. A fascinating subject, I'll say. We'll approach it through the historical context. You know how important it is to understand the power relations among the central and eastern European powers. The repercussions of the Reformation and the Thirty Years' War. The History of Poland and Russia. The different communities, this community, that community. The snow. A good hot coffee. The branches of the maple tree are bowed. The snow swirls outside the windows. Bread with cream cheese and smoked salmon. Dozens of books. The cat purrs by the stove. Mama spreads goose fat on kimmel bread. The Jews, as described by the contemporary Ukrainian writer Galatowski, were exultant.

> The foolish Jews rejoiced, and expected that the Messiah would take them to Jerusalem on a cloud. . . . they fasted several days in the week because of the Messiah, and some fasted the whole week. They gave no food even to their little children, and they immersed themselves in winter under the ice while reciting recently invented prayers. . . . Even some fools among the Christian masses acted and thought like them.

That's it. Emphasize the carnivalesque, the picaresque, the roving, the messianic tohubohu on the roads of eastern Europe, the multicoloured stuff of this wandering humanity. Make them feel for themselves what it meant to a simple soul in the depths of Belorussia or Volhynia to be waiting for the Messiah in total belief in his coming. The hunger for the absolute. The snow, the constant fine, scarcely perceptible flakes. Natasha, as soon as it stops snowing, I'll come pay you a visit. It's true your gravestone is falling into ruin and that it costs a fortune, but I don't like to go a week without saying hello and talking with you. The cat is purring. Mama spreads goose fat on kimmel bread. I come home from violin lesson. The roofs of Vitebsk stand out against the frozen Dvina. I remember lilac colours, green dawns, lemon yellow nights, and black beards. First, make a bibliography, see what they've got lying around in the library, in French, English, Yiddish, Russian, German. Lots of things in Hebrew, I'm sure. Too bad. If I can't cover the subject with five languages, I give up. Start by photocopying the *Encyclopædia Judaica* article on Sabbatai Sevi—that's a good starting point. Then we'll see. Make files, a file on Chmielnicki, one on the mystical movements, one on the geopolitics of central Europe in the period, one on the Ottoman Empire. I'm not very pleased with your work. You didn't make much effort this week. You don't even know who the ally of the great Khan of the Crimea was. Review it. Look at it again.

28

Start again. Does what he can but can't do much—at work—I'll say—and if they don't care, if I'm sent packing because only a couple of crackpots have registered for my course, I'll stay at the pine desk under the window in my long bathrobe, with dozens of books around me, holding my old Bedford pen inscribed R. Cameron, with a good hot cup of coffee and slices of bread with Philadelphia cream cheese and smoked salmon, and organize and reorganize my file cards, make some progress on this text I've been dragging around for so long. Not to feel the cold. Outside, snow all day long. *Suave, mari magno.* The lights of the houses across the street, like the candles in the shacks at the edge of town in Vitebsk. The old shops full of herrings. Morton Himmelfarb sky-colour, a bit wan this morning, colour of a snowy sky, a bit sad, a bit slow—but at least I didn't wake up without a nose like Collegiate Assessor Kovalyov, or transformed into a veritable vermin like poor Gregor Samsa. Nothing like that. Only this damn course that's going to eat up all my time. Redo the whole plan of the twelve classes. Sabbatai Sevi first, maybe. His personal history, three classes. Was he a psychopath? One theory. A homosexual? Another theory. Who was Sarah? Then a flashback to the time of Chmielnicki, Poland, the Ukraine, the Jews—the massacres. Long panoramic view of the corpses. Hordes of orphans on the roads. Spiritual despair of the Jewish communities. Close-up on Chagall's old Jews. Zoom in on their ravaged faces. Another flashback, on Jewish religion and spirituality. Review of the schools of mysticism, the ancient and modern Kabbalah. The Zohar. Abulafia and his "science of the combination of letters." That might interest them. Emphasize it. Don't hesitate to quote Scholem at length:

> The modern reader of these writings will be most astonished to find a detailed description of a method which Abulafia and his followers call *dillug* and *kefitsah,* "jumping" or "skipping" viz., from one conception to another. In fact this is

29

nothing else than a very remarkable method of using associations as a way of meditation. It is not wholly the "free play of association" as known to psychoanalysis; rather it is the way of passing from one association to another determined by certain rules which are, however, sufficiently lax. Every "jump" opens a new sphere, defined by certain formal, *not* material, characteristics. Within this sphere the mind may freely associate. The "jumping" unites, therefore, elements of free and guided association and is said to assure quite extraordinary results as far as the "widening of the consciousness" of the initiate is concerned. The "jumping" brings to light hidden processes of the mind, "it liberates us from the prison of the natural sphere and leads us to the boundaries of the divine sphere."

After all, Freud was a Jew. Perhaps a short digression on these questions. The jump. Everything jumps—Abulafia's letters; Sabbatai, who jumps from Smyrna to Constantinople, from Salonica to Jerusalem; the Jews who jump onto flying carpets to get to their messiah faster; the sultan who makes Sabbatai jump from Judaism to Islam; the Jews who were faithful to Sabbatai and against whom the rabbis issued excommunication orders. History leaps, prances, writhes in laughter and despair. Everything returns to normal, the rabbinical order and persecution by all the Russias. I'm getting off the track. They won't be able to see beyond the surface. I've got to follow chronological order, they need it. Torn apart, pale in the midst of the storm—Natasha, help me—the old asthmatic is failing. Snow on the grave too. Cold the stone and the photo flaking off the monument. You loved small, intimate cemeteries. The one in Tholonnet near Aix-en-Provence —we could have—why run away? Back from the camp—you couldn't go on. The arrest. The big raid. The French all collaborators, you said. You no longer wanted to. Here you have six months of snow on you. You're cold. The ground is frozen hard. You lived on the other side of the Dvina with the leatherworkers and blacksmiths. Blond curls. You were laughing in the storm. The big raid. The French all collaborators, you said, you didn't want to anymore. Sabbatai Sevi marries the Torah. Imagine the scene of the wedding in Salonica. You could even apply the Kabbalistic symbolism and try to describe the colourful atmosphere of the little people of Salonica. Sabbatai Sevi goes to see a psychoanalyst. He has visions, hallucinations. He sees fish everywhere. He carries a fish in a cradle. He grows scales, fins. God. Fish. Imagine a session. Sabbatai Sevi on the couch, talking. You may use Laplanche and Pontalis if you want. Natasha. Fucked up, messed up. Sabbatai Sevi talks about his mother. He loves his mother. He loves only her. She is the Great Whole he wants to merge with. He has no other horizon. No way to break out of this binary relationship. The way of the symbolic is barred. The Kabbalah, the Kabbalah, the Zohar. Fits of euphoria. Deep depressions. Visions. Hallucinations. God of Abraham, God of Isaac, God of Jacob. Tetragrammaton. They banished me from Smyrna. Under the wedding canopy, my bride the Torah. I love you. Three unconsummated marriages. The Torah, my mother. The Torah, my bride. The appeal of the Forbidden, of the devil. The power of darkness. Tetragrammaton. From Smyrna to Salonica. They banished me from Smyrna—to wander among the graves, in Jerusalem, the Pilgrim crossing the sea from Rhodes with its smell of pine trees. Sarah, my mother, Sarah, my wife, Sarah, the Torah. She said she was a survivor of Chmielnicki's massacres, an orphan, from a family that had lived in Podolia for a long time. That a Polish nobleman had mistreated her. Abandoned by everyone, she found herself in Amsterdam. From there to Italy. Didn't the prophet Hosea marry a whore? My mother is dead. I don't know. The Kabbalah. Tetragrammaton. Of course, I won't do anything with it. Cover the traditional material. Tell them far in advance what will be on the exam. Chmielnicki's massacres in eastern Europe. No surprises. The subject will have been dealt with. History is chronology, after all. Sixteen-forty-eight comes before sixteen-sixty-six. Thirty-six hours on Sabbatai Sevi to plan, twelve classes of three hours each. The cat is purring. It's snowing. Vitebsk disappears, becomes fuzzy, wavers. The bulbed churches turn bright purple. Mama spreads goose fat on kimmel bread. Nineteen-thirty comes before today. History sometimes goes berserk. Go over the plan systematically. Start with Jewish mysticism. The Kabbalah. Ibn Gabirol, *chochmah nistarah,* and a stern warning to the first-year students.

> Do not seek what is too difficult for you,
> do not scrutinize what is too strong for you,
> meditate on what is ordered to you, because you have no
> need of secrets.
> Do not interfere with what is beyond your works;
> already you have been shown that which surpasses human
> intelligence.

The sacred name of God, the name possessed by the Shem. The power of the Golem. Show the Wegener film if I can get a suitable room. Rabbi Loew gives life to the Golem, animates it with the *Shem* by putting a magical sign on its chest. Digging a well in an old synagogue, some workers find a statue. They take it to an old antique merchant, who finds the magic formula, tearing from the Kabbalah one of its mysteries. The miracle begins anew, is repeated. The Golem thus becomes the servant of the antique merchant. But he falls in love with the antique merchant's daughter. Rejected, he becomes a blind force. A little girl takes the secret formula from his heart while the monster is asleep, and the Golem once again becomes a mere clay statue. The breath of the *Shem.* That's it. Digression on the Golem and German expressionism. Sabbatai Sevi in the Weimar Republic. A fireman Messiah for 1933, please, to put out the fire in the Reichstag. A returning officer Messiah to change the results of the 1932 elections:

KPD (Communists)	13,779,000	or	37.3%	or the opposite
SPD (Socialists)	7,960,000	or	21.64%	if you
Both left parties together	21,739,000	or	58.94%	wish

have an absolute majority in the Reichstag
or 230 seats for the Communists and
133 seats f or the Socialists or the opposite
total: 363 seats
The NSDAP (Nazis)   5,370,000 votes, or 14.3%

The danger has been averted.

Compulsory reading: Meyrink's *Golem*. A little stroll through the Prague ghetto, Rooster Lane. Crooked roofs, crumbling galleries, dark culs-de-sac, scary lanes.

> An apparition makes its appearance—an utterly strange man, clean shaven, of yellow complexion, Mongolian type, in antiquated clothes of a bygone day; it comes from the direction of the Altschulgasse, stalks through the Ghetto with a queer groping, stumbling kind of gait, as if afraid of falling over, and quite suddenly—is gone.

Go back to Chmielnicki. The action of the Zaporozhya Cossacks. Explain the issues and the Arenda system the Jews were trapped in, the colonization of the lands by the Polish nobility. Bogdan Chmielnicki, who saw himself as the great hetman of an autonomous Ukraine. It's snowing. You loved the snow so much, Natasha. To stay at the pine desk under the window, bundled in a bathrobe, holding the old Bedford pen from New York, surrounded by books, with a good hot coffee and a slice of bread with Philadelphia cream cheese and smoked salmon—old sky-colour feels himself reviving, starting up again. He takes up his crazy text again, his fantastic attempt to revive Sabbatai Sevi. Nothing to do with this crummy course. The imagination races across the Mediterranean basin, rests for a while in Jerusalem, and settles somewhere in eastern Europe in the country of the

Baal Shem—at least that had been the plan, but the text took a tumble, got injured in the crevasses of the unconscious. You will not leave the ghetto. Everything goes back to the last war. In the camp in the snow with my number on my left forearm. Natasha half dead. The return to Paris and our flight. The big raid. The French all collaborators, you said. You didn't want to. Finally get to Sabbatai Sevi. The so-called theological point of view, the psychoanalytic point of view, the psychiatric point of view, the simple historical point of view. An enigmatic character, unknown in spite of the enormous bibliography weighing him down. Perhaps emphasize the period after Sabbatai Sevi, the social movement he started in spite of himself. The epic of Hayim Malakh, the rebel outsider who wanted to depose the sultan and led a caravan of one thousand five hundred people to the Holy Land, where the Messiah was supposed to reappear in 1706. An incredible journey, a wait in vain—it ended badly. The cross or the crescent. The little sect worshipped a wooden statue representing Sabbatai Sevi. Was this mysticism an aberration? No. These rhetorical questions shouldn't be overused, the students don't like it. Just one or two. Make them read. A two-room, I think, I don't see any kitchen. Just a little two-room apartment with the stove in the middle. The cat is purring. It's snowing. I'm coming home from *cheder*, my nose running. My old galoshes leak. My coat doesn't keep me very warm. It's snowing big flakes. I'm coming home from violin class, not *cheder*. Natasha, you liked Babel so much. The weekly visit to the cemetery feels unreal, especially in winter. The mountain seems to float in the air like a rock by Magritte. The gravestones are like the thousand teeth of a monster in the strong wind. In the distance, the line of the Laurentians is a silent Mediterranean. Some days everything is blue; the snow is blue, the ice is blue, my fingers are blue. The maples bent by the wind look like umbrella pines. The cypress poplars lead to your grave. Prewar Nice. Before the camps, before the snow, before the time—before this number on my left forearm. You remember that story by Peretz that you used to tell the neighbours' children?—the soul being judged and the beam even, the two pans exactly level—it had never happened before—and the soul condemned to wander the earth until it can bring the saints in Paradise three gifts worthy of that marvellous place. The story tells how some thieves enter the home of a wealthy Jew and ransack it, and the Jew never loses his composure. They take away gold and silver, jewels and furnishings without our Jew saying anything, even when the leader of the thieves threatens him with a dagger. Suddenly the thieves open a little drawer, and the Jew starts to tremble. "Not that one," he stammers, and the dagger pierces his back. He falls down dead. What was in the drawer? Not gold, not silver, not jewels. There was a little cloth bag containing earth from Palestine that the Jew had wanted to take with him to the grave. That was the first gift the soul brought the saints in Paradise. *Ish hayabi.* Do you remember how well you told these traditional stories in your Belorussian Yiddish with its lilting intonations? Vitebsk is far away, Natasha. You're far away under several feet of snow. Separated. Shortly after your death, I got in the habit of writing you little disjointed notes about everything and nothing. That was nearly twenty years ago. You rejected this country. Nothing but priests, you said. Worse than Spain. Poland, my word, it's Poland. You would have liked to stay in New York. Vitebsk is far away, Natasha—we'll never again see the banks of the Dvina together, or the ochre and pink sunsets soft as silk. But they'd warned me. Don't take the course on Sabbatai Sevi. You've got plenty with the Yiddish course and the one on Mendele Mocher Sforim, traditional courses you prepared a long time ago and give every year. It must be the story I'd hardly started that made me accept this chore. After his conversion to Islam, Sabbatai Sevi, now Aziz Mehmed Effendi, wearing a turban, appointed keeper of the palace gates, awarded a government pension of a hundred and fifty piastres a day in addition to his salary, got into debauchery and stirred up dissident sects of

35

Islam. Heterodox in all religions. Exiled in 1673 to Albania, the ends of the earth, writing "the mysteries of the true faith," he died, it is said, on September 17, 1676, leaving the people of Israel without a messiah, abandoned, in wandering and desolation. That does it for the picturesque part, but I'll also have to cover the details of doctrine. What the orthodox rabbis were fighting. Transfigure Sabbatai Sevi, make him a great thinker, a rebel, almost a revolutionary, an outsider, a deviant. Sabbatai Sevi, our contemporary. Schizo, crackpot, psychotic, borderline, incorrigible shit disturber, winning over the crowds, the poor, those without hope. Doesn't *messiah* come from mess, which means muddle, disorder? Or maybe, play with the time frame, have there be a police report compiled just after Sabbatai's conversion to Islam by some vizier in the pay of Koprili, or by the CIA.

Name: Aziz Mehmed Effendi, formerly known as Sabbatai Sevi

Date of birth: 1626

Domicile: changes frequently—living in Constantinople, native of Smyrna

Occupation: keeper of the palace gates, preacher when the spirit moves him

Civil status: married to a Polish Jewess named Sarah, who is said to be of easy virtue

Identifying marks: to be watched—top priority—dangerous individual—incited unrest among the Jewish population of the Ottoman Empire and far beyond on the roads of Europe past the Euxin bridge—preaches social subversion in his own way—should be removed far from Constantinople if necessary—imminent threat to national security—put a tap on his phone in order to monitor his contacts

Habits:	questionable—said to be sexually deviant, a hypochondriac, undoubtedly schizophrenic —for a long time considered himself the Messiah—a little stay in a seaside rest home would do him a lot of good

It would have been too simple—scarcely arrived, set up as if you'd always been there, everything would be for the best in the best of all possible worlds. This country—opaque. You knew it. You must quickly have realized that one didn't penetrate this place as a scholar, a professional of knowledge, an observer, a journalist, a socio-ethnologist. You must quickly have understood that one didn't enter through conceptual constructions, appearances, or neutralities. No. You must have had to let the language of the body speak. You must have been penetrated by this country, by its light, suckled by its language that is not exactly your own and not exactly another, whipped by its north winds and blowing snow. By chance, by associations, inconsistencies, unexpected meetings, missed appointments, deferred journeys, blunders, misunderstandings, detours, side roads, *Nebenwege.* You must have been snatched up, carried along, devoured willy-nilly. Rebuffed most of the time, rejected—undone, redone. The porousness of the places could invade you—with no order, chronological or logical.

Ségur-Rubinsteins. No *mésalliances.* Your forebears without wedding rings didn't have access to the parlours of Avenue de Ségur. In Longueuil, along a highway:

Fleuriste Pissenlit
Gaz
Pizza Patio
Photo Ste-Foy
Autobody
La Mecque des Sportifs
Vincent Submarines

Pharmacie Claude Lalumière
Tabagie Tremblay
Caisse populaire

Le Fripon restaurant, daily special, complete meal, beverage. Signs, flashers, the city swallowed up, swallowing you up—displaced, deported. Between two seas—but this is no bottle of Entre Deux Mers—hardly an ocean to swallow. Make note of all the differences—the names of the métro stations—the strangeness:

Angrignon
Monk
Jolicoeur
Verdun
De l'Église
LaSalle
Charlevoix
Lionel-Groulx
Atwater
Guy
Peel
McGill
Place des Arts
St-Laurent
Joliette
Pie IX
Viau
L'Assomption
Cadillac
Berri-De Montigny
Beaudry
Papineau
Frontenac
Préfontaine

Langelier
Radisson
Honoré-Beaugrand

What anguish some afternoons. *Québécitude.* Quebecness. I am other. I do not belong to this "we" so often used here, even in the ads. "We." "You." "We should talk to each other." "We're at home here." Another History—the inescapable strangeness. My ancestors did not come here from Poitou or Saintonge or even Paris a very long time ago. They didn't come with Louis Hébert or with Carignan's regiment. I don't have peasant roots. My ancestors weren't *coureurs de bois* confronting danger on faraway portages. I'm not very good at snowshoeing, I don't know the recipes for ragoût de pattes or cipaille. I've never been Catholic. My name is not Tremblay or Gagnon. Even my language breathes the air of another country. We understand and don't understand each other. I'm "coming out of the inn" when you're "not out of the woods yet." Most of all, I do not like Lionel Groulx, I don't like Duplessis, I don't like Henri Bourassa, I'm not stirred by the killing of Father Brébeuf, I've never said my rosary with my family at seven o'clock in the evening. I've never watched the Plouffe family on television. Other, apart, in quarantine—my forties, some grey hairs already—in search of a language, simple words to represent the elsewhere, the density of strangeness, simple words, broken down, tamed, smashed, desemanticized. Image words cutting across several languages. I didn't understand what "ventes sales" were, but they were not "dirty sales." Simple words, not hiding their polysemy to drive you to despair. I am not from here. One doesn't become Québécois. To take the right to speak, to give the right to speak to the immigrants, to their solitude. Give me a smoked meat—a smoked meeting, just as there are boring meetings, or twilight meetings. Twilight blue. It was a blue country. Some days even the snow turned blue. All the eyes in the street were blue. The sky, of course, but also the tongues of sunlight on the glass facades. The clothes of the passers-by, even their faces blue with cold. The country was transformed into a huge blue diamond of a polar city. Blue was also the Quebec flag flapping in the icy wind. Everything was blue. The frozen lakes were blue. Royal blue, turquoise blue, Mediterranean blue. Simple words to represent the everyday difference, speech that is other, multiple. Immigrant words like a cry, like the mauve metaphor of death, voiceless from shouting too much. A country as blue as blueberries, those flower-berries. A fake crêpe Bretonne country.

2070-2102, rue de la Montagne
The gourmet rendezvous
Chez Grandmère—omelettes
Le Colbert—crêpes
À la Crêpe Bretonne
Le Bistrot
La Cabane à Sucre
Le Lancelot
Bar le Cachet
Le Fou du Roi

Crêpes filled with blueberries and gwennerch'h . . $4.95
Crêpes filled with almond paste and whipped cream,
flambéed with kirsch: pride of the house $5.75

Were you less alone in the lively Saturday night crush in the Place de la Contrescarpe? At the foot of your street, bouzoukis and feta, the smell of roast lamb with thyme amid the false laughter. Around eleven o'clock at night, the newspaper seller with the Pakistani accent: *"Hara-kiri, Charlie-Hebdo, Libération, Hara-Kiri, Charlie-Hebdo, Libération."* Were you less alone leaning out the window watching beggars, bums, junkies, lovers, unemployed people, street cleaners, snobs of every kind, depressed intellectuals, and young girls in vintage clothes stroll by? All characters out of a cartoon by Brétecher, starting with you. Everyone to the Chope to cry about the hard times and the cruelty of fate amid the exposed beams and the ski tows at Courchevel. What a show! Even on Sunday, people came to see the house. The long courtyard was separated from the garden next door by a low wall with the coping from an old well in the middle of it. The ivy on the facade faced a tall tree full of birds, and in spring it was like the country, the air buzzing with flies and warm vapours. In the living room across from the kindergarten on the corner of Rue Saint-Médard, the old rebuilt fireplace didn't draw properly. An exquisite apartment whose owner had forgotten to raise the rent. Right in the heart of Paris, your little village. From the Panthéon to Avenue des Gobelins, from Rue de l'Arbalète to Rue Cujas. Beyond . . . across the Seine again, or the Atlantic. Across the bridge—that was the name of a bookstore that no longer exists. Across time. Space full of holes. You knew. That one always longs for Europe of the ancient parapets. No more will you—you said—pick up last-minute items at the Persil Fleuri right across the street. No longer will you line up—you said—at the shop on Rue Blainville run by the woman from Brittany who wanted to force all-those-clowns-who-come-here-and-sit-on-their-asses to get passports. No more will you go to the butcher shop on the square where the butcher always said "voui," instead of "oui," sputtering all over the place.

"A nice escalope please."

"Voui."

"Not too big though."

"Voui."

No more will you go to that crazy bakery where the whole family lisped. No more will you go down the street to the market and be called out to by women telling fortunes with herbs. Sunday mornings in bygone days—the *Mundo Obrero* seller—you came back up the street with two string bags crammed full. Sometimes at Rue de l'Épée-de-Bois there was an old-fashioned brass band, and further up, a barrel organ right out of an old picture book, and still further up, a bum—give me a franc, mam'selle, you wouldn't believe what I can do with a franc—a chunk of bread or a few cigarettes or half a bulb of fennel or a glass of wine. On Rue Saint-Médard right under your windows there was another bum, who was always drunk and who held court every day like Saint Louis under his oak tree. Enthroned on a torn mattress with his back against the wall of the school, he held a telephone found in some trashcan on Rue Descartes and made loud phone calls to God, his mother, Giscard. You had named him Umbilic because of the telephone cord. Umbilic stayed there for hours, in all weather. You saw him in the morning from the kitchen, again at noon, and sometimes even in late afternoon. Umbilic, I'm thinking of you. We're skipping town, Madame. You ache for your travels, for the old dwellings unhabited by you, emptied of your daily life. You knew there are time changes, poles and equators, solstices and equinoxes, icebergs, elsewheres, exiles, impossibilities. You knew. Dilapidated dwellings of Belleville, collapsing walls, empty lots of dreamy childhood, lamp post at the top of the stairs that were in the movie *The Red Balloon*, little interior courtyards, mossy cobblestones, alley cats yawning in sunny windows among pots of geraniums and old wine bottles. Some evenings, the longing. The characters out of the old folklore, from the knife-sharpener to the glazier. I remember a streetcorner that no longer exists. Crooked roofs, crumbling chimneys, zinc eavestroughs, labyrinths silhouetted against the low sky. Violent partings. No more would you go. The porousness of the places haunted you. They were in you, your only identity. You had been that piece of Belleville at the corner of Rue Piat and Rue Vilin. That corner of the Place de la Contrescarpe redolent of fennel and wild thyme, with the ivy sending its tendrils into the bedroom. You had been that house with its extravagant furnishings, the old walnut table, the Spanish secretary, the yew-wood pedestal table, and the Georges III table holding oil lamps and a rustic vase always filled with irises and calendula. You had been that elegant stickiness, that paradise of adulterous loves, curled up, sweaty, heavy. Silence, resounding, talkative, dumbfounded. Paris populace, Paris putrid, Paris garbage pail, Paris tippler, Paris prostitute. You had played in the gutters of Passage Ronce, sending little paper boats down to Rue Julien-Lacroix. You throbbed with that life, with the little holes the ticket-punchers in the métro used to make in the old days before they installed the automatic machines. It wouldn't have taken much to make you too set out to cross the Jardin du Luxembourg with a pack on your back, as in the dictations from Anatole France. The hot chestnuts, the rum crêpes, the roudoudous and coconut candies. You ache for your travels. You knew that—that there are Hundred Years' Wars, Treaties of Versailles, Treaties of Westphalia, Treaties of Utrecht and Rastatt, Italian and German unities, battles of Austerlitz and Sadowa, stormings of the Bastille, of Constantinople, and of the Winter Palace, 1515s, 1789s, 1830s, and 1917s, Julys, Februaries, days in June, sad winters of 1709, little infantas—she's—tiny—a—duenna—takes—care—of—her—she—holds-a-rose-and-looks— Luthers and Calvins, Waterloos, dismal plains, great pains, plain raccoons. Yet today, a thousand miles from your unhabited place, you pick up one of those French history textbooks and you stop at this little detail in a chapter scarcely two pages long, on the Seven Years' War and the Treaty of Paris.

> The struggle also took place in the colonies. But the English takeover of 1755 had made sending reinforcements difficult. Thus the French everywhere were fewer in number than their adversaries. Furthermore, their government considered those distant theatres of operations of secondary importance. As one minister said, "When the house is on fire, you don't worry about the stable." In England, on the other hand, Pitt, who was prime minister from 1757 to 1761, worked hard to promote the war effort. The French had

about ten thousand men in Canada, mainly militiamen recruited among the colonists, supported by "redskin" auxiliaries who were brave but cruel and undisciplined. The English formed lines of up to sixty thousand soldiers. The Canadiens, commanded by a seasoned officer, the Marquis de Montcalm, were unable to prevent the invasion of their country. In 1759, the Englishman Wolfe surrounded Quebec City, which surrendered after a heroic struggle. In 1760, Montreal fell and the Canadien resistance was broken. . . .

On February 10, 1763, the Treaty of Paris settled the conflict over the colonies. France abandoned Canada, the Ohio River Valley, the area east of the Mississippi, a few parcels of land in the Caribbean, and its modest settlements in Senegal to the English. It renounced all territorial claims in India, and kept only five trading posts without being allowed to fortify them: Pondicherry, Chandernagor, Karikal, Yanam, and Mahé. Spain ceded Florida to the English but, in compensation, France, which had gotten Spain into the war, gave Spain Louisiana. This treaty sanctioned the demise of "the first French colonial empire." This disaster appeared at the time to be of little importance as only the tropical territories were considered valuable. In addition, English public opinion expressed a certain disappointment while Choiseul took great pride in having outdone the English by holding on to "the islands." However, England became the dominant colonial and maritime power.

But you're not on a sugar cane island that has become "a *département* of France." For a few acres of snow—you were warned. It isn't a country, it's winter. You'll often look out the window to see if it's melting, when it'll melt, whether it's starting to melt. You'll learn the different qualities of snow, the fine blowing snow that stings your face. You'll see the apocalyptic numbers march across the TV screen on the weather forecast: –10, –15, –17, –20, –25, –27, –32. You'll hear strange words that come from elsewhere: James Bay, Hudson Bay, Baie des Chaleurs, Labrador; Indian names, Kamouraska, Arthabaska,

Abitibi, Shawinigan. Your character must surely have a few contradictions, some weak point. Integrated into the anglophone community but coming from Paris—there must be a lack somewhere. Even her wanderings in the city imply a split. She would get up early in the greyish spring still cool without buds. She would still be wearing her winter boots and hat, maybe her gloves. She would only have traded her heavy winter coat for a lighter leather jacket, over a shapeless wool skirt acquired in a secondhand clothing store in New York. As always on her walks, she would have taken along a book, one or two magazines, her eternal notebook, and her cigarettes and old flint lighter. She would go up on the mountain to the place where you have a view of the whole city. She would stay there for several hours, reading avidly or daydreaming, her gaze fixed on the Saint Lawrence. She would come back down by McTavish and cross the chilly campus to reach the Patisserie Belge, where she would finish out the morning in front of a quiche Lorraine and a green salad. She would smoke a few Gauloises while reading *Le Monde.* The obituary page: "The Lord has seen fit to call to Him Father Louis Bousigues of the parish of Notre-Dame du Raincy, Chevalier of the Legion of Honour, Military Cross 1939–45, who died on July 16, 1979, in his seventieth year. The funeral service will take place at Notre-Dame du Raincy Church, 83 Avenue de la Résistance, on Friday, July 20, at 11 o'clock. Please accept this notice as our personal announcement. For Me Jean Bousigues and the Louvert, Pavel, Laurent, Cousin, Pierre and André Chauffour, Lerasle, Denos, and Saint-Ouen families." The weather: "The unstable cold air mass over the whole country will gradually dissipate. The trough of low pressure in the north of Italy will slowly pass over. The high-pressure system along the Atlantic coast will move in over the western half of France, protecting it from an active zone of new disturbances moving in further north." The *journal officiel,* the stock market reports, the classified ads in which the average apartment went for 50 million old francs. She would go on to the *Nouvel Observateur,* as usual bemoaning the poor quality of the political analysis. Then she would close the magazine and just sit there daydreaming amid the cigarette smoke and the murmur of voices. After her coffee, she would go back out into the brisk air of late winter. Spring would definitely be late again this year. There would still be spots where the remains of the January snow, sad and dirty, refused to disappear. Soon she would turn in the direction of the Université de Montréal. She would go to Renaud-Bray and pick up the paper—*L'Humanité, Le Matin, Le Monde, Le Nouvel Obs*—and would spend a long time looking at the new books, punctuating her explorations with "well, well, so-and-so has gotten published," and "such-and-such book has finally come out," as if the bridges between her and Parisian life had not been burned, as if dialogue were still possible. After an hour, the charms of the bookstore would have palled. She would be hungry. She'd just have to cross Côte-des-Neiges to Chez Vito, and the ritual would begin again. She would take her Gauloises and old flint lighter from her bag and spread out her newspapers and magazines. Munching a Neapolitan pizza, she would get into a rage over an article in *Le Monde,* an editorial by Jean Daniel, or something in *L'Huma,* or laugh out loud at a play on words in *Libé.* Then it would be time for the notebook with the red and black cover. She would fill its pages with poetry in Yiddish, following the inspiration of the moment. From time to time, as she attacked another slice of pizza, a word or an assonance would suddenly strike her or, as her hand moved to the ashtray to stub out a cigarette, an image would take shape, or an analogy, or a comparison; sometimes an entire passage would come to her this way. She would never cross anything out right away. She would wait a few days before rereading it, and then she would work on those images, those words, those arrangements, those structures. She would linger there a long time, musing. La Motte Picquet-Grenelle. The Canon de Grenelle, the noisy grey metal of the elevated métro, the Bouquet de Grenelle, the Bar des Sports, the Pierrot. Wet sidewalks. Paris is disintegrating. It's so far away!

Immigrant words disturb. Their questioning is panting with uncertain answers. No solutions. Stammering, gauche, left-wing, no class, classified in police files. The words hit home, shatter the obvious like a stone against a mirror. Words of sun or of distant plains, fig words, olive words, woman words—you won't let them make you toe the line, you will not fall into LINE. No trespassing—no passing away—Pascal supplies—supplications—tantalizations—palpitations—pale ale—the Pale—*t'chum hamoishev*—a room for Moishe—Moishe's pit—Babi Yar—black hole—rage. Have I really left it? She too, my character, should know perfectly well that the *shtetl* no longer exists. The ghetto—the war—the sirens—reigns the queen of Sheba—the Sabbath queen—but there's no Sabbath any more. Immigrant words travel across language—the voice of elsewhere—the voice of the dead. They pierce. Her wanderings are like the slow flights between two raids. She would never know where her steps would take her. From now on, the time of between. Between two cities, between two languages, between two cities, two cities in one city. Between—the parentheses that in Yiddish are called half-moons. Inside the half-moons. Half-honeymoons, half May moons. Half-full moons. In the half-moons. Torn between cultures I'm astraddle: Crescent Street, Rue St-Denis, Victoria Avenue. To change one's skin, language, food, time, sex, name. The anguish of the proper name when it's lost, when it changes, when the everyday signifier, the mark, the insignia, the signature change. My new one rings like the sea crossed and the mother lost. The only link, the only country, my mother. You lost—again to wander. We have always been wanderers. *Immer.* Always. *Himmel* the sky. The loss of name, mother, place. Without home or hearth, without warmth. Real or fictive pasts, I have lost you. Nowhere—Pitchipoi—not here either. Once upon a time there would be an immigrant. She would have come from far away, never having been at home. She would continue her running with her wandering Jew's stick and her star, under the stars, with her train of traditional images, worn-out stereotypes. She would continue to see the birth of new languages, listening. In spite of. Once upon a time there was the Passage Ronce in Belleville. What remains of it, the trace of a street sign. The bricks are darker in that spot. Above the trace, "20th arrondissement" on a curved piece of blue sign, and below the trace, "Private road. No vehicles over 2000 kg. Trespassers will be held responsible for damage." After La Motte Picquet, I don't know any more. Why these disjointed words, even in their pain spread out naked, awkward? The broken words of the foreigner, the archaic chants of elsewhere. Along the streets that look alike, Sherbrooke between REGENT and the west end one Friday afternoon.

CITY AND DISTRICT SAVINGS BANK
SUTTON PASTRY DELICATESSEN
CHARCOAL STEAKS RESTAURANT
BROADWAY GROCERY   MONSIEUR HOT DOG
CANADA DRY   ROYAL BANK
TORONTO DOMINION
BCN
CANTOR'S BAKERY
HITACHI
PEPSI
CINÉMA KENT
CROWN CARPET
TCHANG KIANG restaurant chinois
PERRETTE
SOUVLAKI
TITO ESPRESSO BAR
PRIMO
HANDY ANDY quincaillerie

You'd say it was New York, the New York of the poor, rundown. My own NY. That of my imaginary parents who arrived at

Ellis Island in the 1920s. She would like greasy hamburgers with mustard, sweet relish, and ketchup. Washed down with a coke. Disgusting. And the so-called regular coffee, coffee-coloured dishwater, she'd like it. This laissez-faire, this no-man's-land would be hers. She would feel at home in the midst of this obese crowd in their loud, poorly made clothes. After Grenelle—I don't know any more, the line gets lost in my memory.

They would have integrated into Montreal's Jewish community. They would celebrate Purim, Chanukah, Rosh Hashanah, Yom Kippur. They would read the *Vorwarts* and the *Jewish Chronicle*. They would write for *Commentary* or even the *Gazette*. They'd attend every lecture or activity at the Saidye Bronfman Centre, they would be members of the Jewish Public Library. They'd often eat at the Brown Derby with Mime Yente. A soft life without any explosions. In the summer they would go to Israel, to Natanya, to a country house they had rented for a long time, for which they'd save all year. And in the winter, sometimes, to Miami, to Yente's relatives. It would have been good to go on like that indefinitely. No longer to have the CIA or the RCMP or the Deuxième Bureau on their case. Good citizens, right-thinking, voting for Goldbloom provincially. An ordinary conformity. Just like everyone else. One country, one flag, one anthem—*La Marseillaise, Hatikvah,* or *O Canada,* but something, at the top of their lungs, in unison. Solemn ceremonies, inaugurations, minutes of silence, flag raisings, monuments to the dead. Monumental lies to the dead. Not a single false note—let's march in step, all for one. Note all the differences. Note everything.

On the Main   boulevard St-Laurent
    Schwartz Montreal Hebrew Delicatessen
     Duty Prepared Parcels for USSR
  The Main St. Lawrence Steak House
    Voyage OVNIK
     WARSHAWA

B.B.Q. Jorbel
　　Charcuterie portugaise
　Berson et fils monuments
　Bar BQ Cocorico　ZAGREB Delicatessen.

A second-rate America thrown together pell-mell. Times
and places, all countries, all Histories, all peoples compressed.
An ecumenism of the poor, the hunted, those with no right to
speak. Pell-mell. Fragmented. The America of always. Not a
country. Imaginations, longings. Remakes, ersatz. To be at the
edge, at the door, at the threshold, and nobody to ask you to
come in—elsewhere—a pilgrim without a goal. Elijah come back
disguised as a beggar, an immigrant. Yes, that would be good.
She asked everyone the way. They all wanted to help her but
she didn't know where she was going, where she would go.
She asked them for her country, but it didn't exist, having been
forgotten by God on the day of creation. A country without a
History, without dates, without treaties, without masters and
without servants. It was easy to lose the path on the mountain.
After a few miles, there was no more path. It says in Ansky's
Dybbuk that every morning at dawn, the Eternal One grieves over
the destruction of the Temple, and his tears fall on the doorsteps
of synagogues. And that's why the oldest ones have rustlings in
the walls. But synagogues and the tears of the Eternal One had
nothing to do with her. What about her tears? Who would dry
them?

For centuries, separated from herself, banished, infidel,
witch, heretic, violated, whipped, imprisoned. The ghetto also
within her making her hunch herself up, curl herself very small
like a cat, a ball, like that soul flying from world to world in search
of its clothes, its costumes, its masks. In Hebrew, between the
face and misfortune there is only a *vav* of difference, a little verti-
cal line, and between the dead and the Messiah only a single en-
tity, the *sh* of ssh . . . of the silence of speech stopped.

She would continue to give courses on Babel in Jewish Studies at McGill for a starvation wage.

"A Pole closed my eyes," whispered the old man, in a voice that was barely audible. "The Poles are bad-tempered dogs. They take the Jew and pluck out his beard, the curs! And now they are being beaten, the bad-tempered dogs. That is splendid, that is the Revolution. And then those who have beaten the Poles say to me: 'Hand your phonograph over to the State, Gedali . . .' 'I am fond of music, Pani,' I say to the Revolution. 'You don't know what you are fond of, Gedali. I'll shoot you and then you'll know. I cannot do without shooting, because I am the Revolution.'"

"She cannot do without shooting, Gedali," I told the old man, "because she is the Revolution."

"But the Poles, kind sir, shot because they were the Counter-Revolution. You shoot because you are the Revolution. But surely the Revolution means joy. And joy does not like orphans in the house. Good men do good deeds. The Revolution is the good deed of good men. But good men do not kill. So it is bad people that are making the Revolution. But the Poles are bad people too. Then how is Gedali to tell which is Revolution and which is Counter-Revolution? I used to study the Talmud, I love Rashi's Commentaries and the books of Maimonides. And there are yet other understanding folk in Zhitomir. And here we are, all of us learned people, falling on our faces and crying out in a loud voice: 'Woe unto us, where is the joy-giving Revolution?'"

The old man fell silent. And we saw the first star pierce through the Milky Way.

"The Sabbath has begun," Gedali stated solemnly, "Jews should be going to the synagogue." . . .

The Sabbath is passing. Gedali, the founder of an impossible International, has gone to the synagogue to pray.

The *shtetl* is passing. The *shtetl* is gone. And Gedali and you and Babel and lots of others. Gedali, Gedali, even here in Montreal in this America of delicatessens, black bread, pickles, pickled herring, even here, Gedali, I look for the *shtetl* without finding it. Lost on the Main, on St-Urbain, or on Roy, she persisted in asking for Novolipie Street, Gesia Street, Leszno Street, Franciskana Street. She confused places, periods, languages, and peoples. She was unable to understand, to admit, that it was all over. Finished. *Judenrein.* All over. Even here in Montreal, the *shtetl* is gone, Gedali, and gone also our dreams. Gedali, Gedali, the Sabbath is passing.

NOT   SO   FAST

A quiet milieu, blind to anything that doesn't directly concern it. Contributing to Israel and Begin's policies, spewing the USSR new arch-enemy, always backing the States, aiding Somoza and South Africa. Impeccable logic, a relentless progression from the moment they choose their camp. Closed to left-wing struggles. Not interested in the Palestinians or the people's struggle, becoming dominators, exploiters, torturers. Acting like the others. A state like any other, with its police, its Deuxième Bureau, its intelligence and counter-intelligence service, its wiretapping, its censorship, its hierarchies. A people like any other with its geniuses, its thieves, its ministers, and its whores. The return to ordinary humanity. An anthem, a flag, embassies, representatives—the wheels of History. Sobbing—in pieces—adrift. There's a part of me dreaming in some border kibbutz deserted by the young. Another part of me on the Palestinian side doesn't hesitate to attack that same kibbutz where I stand guard armed in the night. A puzzle of History with some pieces missing, that can never be completely put back together. From now on, the time of elsewhere, between-three-languages, between-two-alphabets, between-two-oceans, between-two-worlds, between-two-logics, between-two-longings. Because there would be strange longings. Her real country, Kasrilevke, Sholom Aleichem's imaginary town —her own world, which she would not have known, which she could not get free of. Or stories that never ended, always the same, told by a bearded old man. Children, come to the table, quickly, says the great-grand-father in a cracked voice, relighting the candle. They hurry in, arrange the chairs. One pokes a log in the fireplace and brings the fire back to life, because it's cold and their coats aren't very heavy. The old man is going to search his memories and tell a story, and the wind of Volhynia, the icy breath of the white desert, will be forgotten. In those days, a very long time ago, he begins, there reigned a man who was said to be the cruelest tyrant Russia ever had. They all shiver. Not long ago, they survived a pogrom. The youngest had his head split open, and the scar still shows. Was there a worse tyrant than Nicholas II? Undoubtedly, because the old great-grandfather says so. God, why don't you choose another people. Give us a little peace. Just a little. It was in the reign of Nicholas I, the bloody czar, the military czar. It is he who is said to have conceived the terrible Cantonist system. You don't know what the Cantonist system is? The children gesture no, opening their sad eyes wide. I'm going to tell you about the *rekruchina* I myself got caught in. A very long time ago, Jews didn't do any military service. They paid a special tax. This was a heavy burden on the communities, but at least the Jews didn't have to go into the devil's army. One day, Nicholas I decided to conscript Jews into the army. These Jews had to be eighteen years old and they had to do twenty-five years of service. The children held their breath. Twenty-five years? Yes, twenty-five years. At the end of that time, if they were still alive, they were given a piece of land somewhere in central Asia far from the *shtetl*. In the meantime, in their misery and isolation, they would have forgotten their religion and their language. The Jewish communities themselves had to provide the conscripts or else they would be severely punished. Often there were not enough young men, and they conscripted children twelve years old, eight years old. We lived in a *shtetl* near Zhitomir, a few *versts* from here. I must have been—let me see—he searches his memory in a painful effort to remember —let me see, ten years old. I was little and sickly, and I was all my mother had. I was in the forest looking for dead wood to burn for heat when I was captured by a band of "beaters." I hardly remember it any more. They put a grey coat on me that was much too big and I found myself marching in ranks with some fifty boys like me. We were cold, we were tired. Our masters were hostile, shouting all the time. They threatened us, ridiculed us, demanded that we convert to the Orthodox religion. I decided to run away at the first opportunity. I was angry at the *shtetl* authorities who allowed the poor people to be enlisted. I remember a song from later, much later.

> They grab them at school,
> Put a grey coat on them.
> And our advisers, our rabbis . . .

> Rich Mr. Rochover has seven children—
> Not one is in uniform.
> Leah the poor widow only has one kid—
> They hunted him down like a wild animal.

> Is it right to recruit among the poor?
> Shoemakers and tailors, all they've got are their poor skins.
> But the children of the elegant rich man
> Can keep going. They lack for nothing.

Yes, I must have been ten. We marched for days and days, our lips blue, our eyes sad, so exhausted we were scarcely able to talk. We crossed Volhynia, the Ukraine. When we got to the Crimea, half the contingent had died. I was very sick myself. I was losing hope. I saw no salvation either in fleeing—I was too weak to get very far—or in submitting to conversion. I had heard that some boys who had renounced their faith had later been slaughtered, but no one knew exactly who had done it.

In spite of everything, I managed one day to escape into the mountains of the Crimea. The children's eyes opened wide, feverish. I became a woodcutter in a remote village in the region of Tauris. In the evenings, I often thought of my poor companions and my mother back in Volhynia. I saw the wooden house with its high windows and painted wood shutters again. The bright blue skies of the Crimea didn't succeed in making me forget the big clouds of the plains with their fields of poppies as far as the eye can see. My Volhynia, dark and earthy. I yearned— I wanted to kill the czar. A very long time after, I came back to the *shtetl* as a pedlar. My mother had been dead for many long years. Hardly anyone recognized me. I set out on the road again. I never became a Cantonist again. Children, never forget the old Cantonist.

This longing would also come back in poems, scraps of stories, proverbs, sayings, but with something of death in the colour of the false memory. Keeping relics alive? A cult of the dead? After the flood? "And the flood was forty days upon the earth; and the waters increased, and bare up the ark, and it was lift up above the earth. And the waters prevailed, and were increased greatly upon the earth; and the ark went upon the face of the waters. And the waters prevailed exceedingly high upon the earth; and all the high hills, that were under the whole heaven, were covered. Fifteen cubits upward did the waters prevail; and the mountains were covered. And all flesh died that moved upon the earth, both of fowl, and of cattle, and of beast, and of every creeping thing that creepeth upon the earth, and every man: All in whose nostrils was the breath of life, of all that was in the dry land, died. And every living substance was destroyed which was upon the face of the ground, both man, and cattle, and the creeping things, and the fowl of the heaven; and they were destroyed from the earth: and Noah only remained alive, and they that were with him in the ark. And the waters prevailed upon the earth an hundred and fifty days." But God made a mistake in his accounting. From November 15, 1940, the day the Warsaw ghetto was sealed off, until the end of 1943, there were nearly a thousand days—a thousand days of dying—and what Noah to survive?

AFTER GRENELLE—I DON'T KNOW ANY MORE
THE LINE GETS LOST
                    IN MY MEMORY
                Jews
                must
                use
                the
                last
                car.
It was nice out on July 16, 1942
           around Rue DR FINLAY
                Rue NOCARD
                Rue NELATON
AROUND GRENELLE. The 15th arrondissement.
           WURDEN   VERGAST
The operation was called
                SPRING WIND
HER MOTHER—NEVER RETURNED
SHE LATER IN AMERICA
                WURDEN VERGAST
     Near GRENELLE
GEDALI   WHO REMEMBERS?

They would spend their weekends in all seasons walking in
the city, dreaming of buying a house in Hampstead, NDG, or
Westmount. There would be ecstasies, raptures, cries of joy and
desire, invariably ending in swearing. "All those idiots in these
beautiful houses—why isn't it us?" Front galleries, bay windows,
gables, Edwardian roofs, alcoves, sculpted details. Nothing would
be left to chance. They would see everything. Avidly, greedily.
They would regularly pace the heights of Westmount and Côte-
St-Antoine, coming back, rueful, by way of Grosvenor and Circle
Road, and they'd set their heart on different types of homes de-
pending on their mood. It might be the seventeenth century

Hurtubise house on Côte-St-Antoine, a wood house, raised because of the snow, with a beautiful gallery and dormer windows and tall chimneys, surrounded by trees and flanked by an old barn. She would immediately have begun to imagine how those large rooms, with their elegant woodwork fastened with hand-forged nails, should be decorated, or what furniture would go with the rough-hewn cedar beams. Or they might become anti-social and dream of isolation—but in the middle of the city—and the house at 474 Mount Pleasant, built on the slope of the mountain, in the American style, covered with shingles, hidden in the trees, spacious, rustic but comfortable, would fit this wish for a false escape perfectly. Another time, it might be a Queen Anne house on Elm Avenue that would delight them with its pink stone Egyptian facade, its octagonal tower reminiscent of the crusades, its ornate windows and porch and wrought iron railings along the front steps. Yes, Elm Avenue, right near Atwater, the métro, the centre. They would dream, make plans. "Our room will be on the second floor, and the living room on the first floor." He would agree, happy to see her so childlike and impractical. He, who would have lived on Upper Broadway in a miserable hovel across from Columbia, would have a hard time imagining himself a landlord on Elm Avenue in Westmount. Still another time, it might be the brick house painted white and grey like those in New England, at the corner of Grosvenor and Westmount Avenue. A nice exposure, tranquility, opulence. One day, no longer able to resist, they would have made the rounds of the real estate agents:

A.E. LEPAGE
ROYAL TRUST
MONTREAL TRUST
FRANK NORMAN
LE PERMANENT

Back from their brunch at the Snowdon Delicatessen, he would have opened *The Gazette* and, laughing, said: "Listen, here are some houses for us. 'Upper Westmount. First advertisement, central air conditioning, 3 plus 1 bedrooms, 4½ bathrooms, 3 log-burning fireplaces, lovely pine-panelled playroom, 2-car garage, nice patio and garden, super condition, near Devon Park. MLS $164,500. Telephone . . . .'

"'Upper Westmount, 9 Summit Circle. Modern, 5 bedrooms, 4½ bathrooms, central air conditioning, double garage, very bright, lovely views. MLS $265,000.'

"Another one. 'Private sale. Elegant detached home facing beautiful park, near private schools, beautiful oak woodwork and floors. Ideal for entertaining. 3 fireplaces, 3 bathrooms, 2 powder rooms, modern kitchen, 6 bedrooms, den on main floor. $235,000.'"

Finally the last one, because they would be laughing too hard to go through the rest of the section. "'Classic stone residence, 12 rooms, separate living and dining rooms, private master bedroom suite with adjoining full bath. Charming modern kitchen, double garage. $300,000. Telephone . . . .'"

They would have called one of the agents and put on their best clothes. For once he would have taken off his perennial jeans and had his hair trimmed; she would have put on makeup. They would have been taken seriously. A nice young couple, well off, carefree, wanting to establish a good solid home. They would have spent the day visiting houses with large living rooms, big fireplaces redolent of birch wood, African hangings, paintings, bathrooms out of a Hollywood movie, carpets soft as moss. Tired of all this inaccessible luxury (she would have calculated that their savings for two years would barely buy them a quarter of a bathroom), they would have told the agent at the end of the day that they needed to think about it and talk to their family and friends. He would have said this in English with a very refined university accent. The agent would have taken this for enthusiasm. They would have gotten over all this unreality in a little Spanish restaurant, where they would be joined by an old friend from Vienna. They would have ordered sangria and paella with shrimps. "First of all, that kind of life isn't for us. We're petty-bourgeois. We'd probably become impossible. We'd become stay-at-homes, we'd water our plants and we wouldn't think about anything any more. No more political activism." She would have lighted a Gauloise, shrugging. As if you could be a political activist here! He would have replied a little curtly, "But there's lots to do here. If you want to be active. The MCM, women's groups, all kinds of community groups, the Human Rights Commission, the unions. After all, the CSN isn't exactly George Meany, is it? There's the movement for secular schools, since you can't stand the church; there are all the immigrant groups; there are Communists, Maoists, even the Trots; there are the gays; there are writers' groups. There's even the PQ. There's anything you want. And you'd be welcome." She wouldn't have said anything, ashamed of her obvious Eurocentrism, her Euro-communism, her inability sometimes to go beyond the narrow confines of her Parisian culture. There would be a silence among the three of them then. The Viennese friend would have broken it by ordering two more pitchers of sangria. They would each have spoken their little piece of nostalgia real or imaginary, spontaneous or long practised, touching on all the cities of Europe.

"I know an incredible brothel in Venice."

"Ah, Venice, the domes of La Salute."

"The city is slowly sinking into the silt, as in a dream."

"I know a restaurant in Budapest, on the hill, one the tourists don't know about, where you can drink a Badascony."

"Really."

"Ah, Budapest."

"The Danube, the Chain Bridge, Margaret Island!"

"In Prague, in Malá Strana, there's an inn on a little three-cornered square with an old well and a linden tree—I think

Apollinaire lived there—with old beams and a big fireplace and freshly cut flowers and tables that smell of furniture polish. Ah, Prague with its rosy fingers, the golden city, the baroque city. Waiter, more sangria!"

"None of that compares to Vienna, around the Hofburg. Franz Joseph's favourite tea room, where they have the best strudel in the world."

"Ah, Vienna, with its lilacs, its fragrance—and Freud's house!"

And the evening would have flowed like the sangria, like the blood in their veins. Exiles, foreigners, always elsewhere. Berlin. The Berlin they spoke of with tears in their eyes would have been an imaginary Berlin—Valentin, the cabarets, Brecht, the expressionists, the Depression, the Spartacists, Berlin before the rise of fascism.

"Ah, Berlin, around the Alexanderplatz."

"Ah, Rosa."

A house in Berlin, in Vienna, in Prague, in Budapest, in Venice.

"It's all over, the dreams of houses," she would have declared, already half tipsy. "Even if the English leave, even if house prices go down, we'll never have a house unless we win the Olympic lottery."

And they would have laughed, glad to be together, to be able to call up all these names from central Europe, and somehow glad also to be Jewish. She would have started to sing. *Ich bin von Kopf bis Fuss auf Liebe eingestellt,* Marlene Dietrich's song in *Der Blaue Engel,* and all three would have sung the refrain, enjoying their closeness. She would have broken the mood of well-being.

"You know what we're like?" she would have asked. "At the end of Flaubert's *Sentimental Education,* Frédéric Moreau meets an old friend from his adolescence and they recall their youth, the joys and sorrows they shared. They reminisce about the time they went to a brothel and Frédéric says it was 'the happiest time we ever had.' 'Yes,' the friend says, 'it was the happiest time we ever had.' That's what we're like. We go on about central Europe between the wars. Yes. And all that leads to Auschwitz, as you know."

"But," says the Viennese friend, "doesn't Freud say at the end of one of his books, quoting Scripture, that it isn't forbidden to limp?"

You don't have to be Jewish to love Cantor's bagels.

Schizophrenic city.

You don't have to be Québécois to love Gilles Vigneault, snowshoeing, and Lac-St-Jean tourtière.

Words mutilated

Words crossed

Words cut

words from beyond, from beyond-memory, words of lack. You don't have to. Words have no shadows, no halos, no coronas. De Chirico's words, or Delvaux's words, or Magritte's words. At the edge of words.

Once there were countries of lavender, summers, purple skies, warm nights.

You don't have to   pas besoin

wandering can't be placed, like that voice in the Bible that's neither God nor Moses. An unidentifiable voice, without a name or an echo.

Once upon a time in New York in a ratty Chock Full o' Nuts on Upper Broadway across from Columbia, there was a mad linguist, or a linguist madman, with a Greek newspaper in one hand and a German-Italian dictionary in the other, speaking in English to whoever was willing to serve as his public. "Tell me, would you say *spaghetti* comes from Italian or Chinese?" Talking nonstop.

And further on, a bum who had found an old battery-run tape recorder in a trashcan on 110th Street and was trying to make it work, talking to himself, laughing, crying all alone in the New York misery of a still-mild late December between two murders in Morningside Park and the carefree joggers on Riverside, amid the smell of bagels and the one-dollar breakfast special. One doesn't cross borders. One passes over them. They have no transparency. They are traps. One falls into them bag and baggage. On the other side, words are no longer the same colour. You've always lived beyond borders, in a language, a language along the roads of central Europe where once the poppies and columbine and fall mushrooms spoke Yiddish, where the clouds still play the fiddle on evenings stitched up in the back of the courtyards of Warsaw or Vilna. A trace of the *shtetl* in Montreal or New York, barely perceptible. America winks, blind in one eye, scabrous.

> Fish and chips
> Donuts
> Steak house
> McDonald
> Coffee House
> Howard Johnson
> Hamburger—Cheeseburger—Steerburger
> Club sandwich
> Hot dogs
> Coke—Pepsi—7-Up
> Kentucky Fried Chicken
> Hilton
> Sheraton
> Holiday Inn

I will go dressed in sackcloth with ashes on my head, holding the Book of Job, I will go and mourn the great bereavement of the ghetto lost.

Schizophrenic city
split
torn

Taking the 24 bus from beginning to end along Sherbrooke, that endless street, a chameleon street, a jungle street. First the shops of NDG, low buildings with bazaar storefronts and signs that not very long ago were still completely in English. Charming little residential streets of single-family brick houses meet them at right angles. Toward the east, after Décarie, there's more activity, more expensive stores, tall houses, banks. This is the Sherbrooke of florist shops, of Murray's, and of Clément's with its lobsters and apple pies. Then the Sherbrooke of Westmount stretching to Atwater—spacious brick or stone houses with cornices and gables, Victorian dwellings with big gardens you imagine in back, parks, tidy avenues, cheerful spaces full of joggers and children. The street becomes livelier again at Greene, passes more parks, gardens, and Victorian and Edwardian residential buildings, and becomes temporarily quiet at Côte-des-Neiges. Between Côte-des-Neiges and St-Laurent, the street changes into downtown, into a street of banks, luxury shops, restaurants, grand hotels, skyscrapers, office towers, and art galleries, a Sherbrooke that's the Avenue de l'Opéra and Rue Saint-Honoré all in one. The Sherbrooke of the rich people who shop at Holt Renfrew, live in Le Chateau, and eat at the Ritz-Carlton, of the professionals who lunch on Rue de la Montagne, of the McGill students who emerge from the campus at McTavish. A Place de la Bourse Sherbrooke, a Sherbrooke of the *grands boulevards*. Then the high-rise buildings thin out, giving way to townhouses and posher restaurants as you approach Rue St-Denis—this town's Latin Quarter—and Rue St-Hubert. Further east, the fabric gets shabby. It's the Sherbrooke of the poor, of molasses, of the lower city, of petroleum, of factories. The Sherbrooke where one never goes, where only French is spoken, the sad Sherbrooke, where the snow is grey even right after a storm, where thoughts are grey as life. A garbage-dump Sherbrooke, a discounted Sherbrooke, a Sherbrooke of no account. The same street for nearly sixty miles, two or three universes where you don't belong. Wandering has a thousand faces in which you do not see yourself.

> Schizophrenic city
> collage of languages
> ethnic stew full of lumps
> purée of crushed cultures
>> turned into folksy clichés
>>> frozen
>>> pizza
>>> souvlaki
>>> paella

Italy is far, Greece is far. Spain is far. Everything is congealed in grease, oil, American margarine. You put sweet Kraft dressing on your salad. Forgetting starts with the taste of the food, the colour of the sky, the sound of the voices, the smell of the streets. Who remembers the Piazza Navona, Las Ramblas of Barcelona, the lanes of Athens? Who remembers the Warsaw ghetto? Or before the Warsaw ghetto? Before time, before History? LOVE IT OR MAPLE LEAVE IT—undesirable aliens, all of them communists, all subversives, all revolutionaries.

Revolutionary and stationary, left behind by time.

Reduced to silence, to wandering, to the loss of their History, their memory, imprisoned in myth. Note all the differences, especially the NHL hockey scores because the Canadiens are catching up and will definitely win the Stanley Cup again.

The newspaper, Thursday, January 17, 1980.

NATIONAL HOCKEY LEAGUE

Tuesday
N.Y. Islanders 5, Winnipeg 2
Philadelphia 7, Washington 4
St. Louis 2, Minnesota 1

Yesterday
Montreal at Chicago
Boston at Quebec City
Winnipeg at N.Y. Range
Atlanta at Vancouver
Edmonton at Washington
Toronto at Pittsburgh
Colorado at Detroit
Buffalo at Los Angeles
St. Louis at Minnesota

Today
Toronto at N.Y. Islanders
Chicago at Philadelphia
Atlanta at Colorado
Pittsburgh at Hartford
Edmonton at Boston

Scoring leaders
(not including
yesterday's games)

	G	A	P
Dionne, LA	36	54	90
Lafleur, Mtl	32	46	78
Taylor, LA	30	42	74
Simmer, LA	36	33	69
Trottier, NYI	26	34	60
Gretzky, Edm	22	38	60
Federko, SL	17	39	56
Perreault, Buff	29	23	52
Larouche, Mtl	29	23	52
Gare, Buff	28	22	50

Friday
Detroit at Winnipeg
Buffalo at Vancouver

QUEBEC MAJOR JUNIOR HOCKEY LEAGUE

Tuesday
Montreal 6, Shawinigan 5
Chicoutimi 5, Quebec City 2
Trois-Rivières 12, Hull 2

Yesterday
Sherbrooke at Hull

Today
Trois-Rivières at Cornwall
Chicoutimi at Sorel

Friday
Chicoutimi at Montreal
Verdun at Shawinigan
Quebec City at Sherbrooke

NATIONAL HOCKEY LEAGUE

	GP	W	L	T	GF	GA	Pts
1 – PHILADELPHIA	42	28	3	11	179	129	67
2 – BUFFALO	43	28	12	3	164	118	59
3 – BOSTON	41	23	12	6	155	120	52
4 – MINNESOTA	40	21	11	8	168	121	50
5 – MONTREAL	44	22	16	6	164	147	50
6 – LOS ANGELES	42	20	14	8	181	161	48
7 – N.Y. RANGERS	45	20	17	8	173	162	48
8 – CHICAGO	43	17	14	12	122	125	46
9 – PITTSBURGH	42	17	14	11	146	144	45
10 – ST. LOUIS	44	18	19	7	138	143	43
11 – N.Y. ISLANDERS	41	18	17	6	143	134	42
12 – TORONTO	41	18	19	4	150	158	40
13 – QUEBEC CITY	42	17	19	6	132	145	40
14 – ATLANTA	41	16	20	5	136	147	37
15 – VANCOUVER	44	15	22	7	139	151	37
16 – DETROIT	41	14	20	7	135	141	35
17 – WINNIPEG	45	13	27	5	118	174	31
18 – HARTFORD	40	10	20	10	128	152	30
19 – EDMONTON	41	10	22	9	139	179	29
20 – COLORADO	42	12	25	5	138	165	29
21 – WASHINGTON	42	11	25	6	131	163	28

QUEBEC MAJOR JUNIOR HOCKEY LEAGUE
Lebel Division

	GP	W	L	T	GF	GA	Pts
CORNWALL	48	25	21	2	250	239	52
MONTREAL	47	23	22	2	236	261	48
HULL	47	14	26	7	214	272	35
SOREL	45	14	27	4	234	266	32
LAVAL	48	10	34	4	192	321	24

Dilio Division

	GP	W	L	T	GF	GA	Pts
CHICOUTIMI	47	32	13	2	306	218	66
SHERBROOKE	47	29	14	4	284	210	62
TROIS-RIVIERES	48	26	15	7	302	215	59
QUEBEC CITY	47	24	19	4	228	230	52
SHAWINIGAN	48	18	24	6	210	224	42

a Quebec   of Coke
a Quebec   of french fries
a Quebec   of toast, relish, ketchup
           eggs over easy with bacon
a Quebec   of credit cards
           American Express
           Chargex
           MasterCharge
           Diners Club
a Quebec   of multinational petroleum
           corporations
                     Texaco
                     Shell
                     Esso
                     Gulf Oil
           with profits of 100% sometimes
it's for the good of all of you
and since you're dumb enough to believe it
a rich, white Puerto Rico
51st star in the American flag with a *fleur de lys*
     for extra soul
                Ici on parle français
                     and
                we think American
                we think Trilateral
           national security with
     crucifixes in the schools
for a good cause
     In God we trust—so do we, thank you—
not to mention the holy martyrs canonized in 1930.
     We'll all go to Florida this winter, or Acapulco.
A few trade unionists in prison here and there
                They should have behaved themselves.
     a Quebec   of Molson's

a Quebec   of Labatt's
a Quebec   of Pepsi
            colony
and you lost in the midst of all this sound
                and fury
                without a voice
                words defeated
                words forgotten
                words deformed
                words displaced
                words deported
words from beyond space. They have no place any
more. I will go dressed in sackcloth with ashes on
my head, holding the Book of Job, I will go and
mourn the great bereavement of words lost.

            Voiceless in Quebec
            Yet still privileged
even though they don't want anything to do with you
        even though they remind you every day that
                you're not from here
        Still privileged
        Imagine.
You come from Portugal. You have four children.
Your husband took off shortly after your arrival.
You work in a garment factory
at the minimum wage. You're a job stealer.
            Voleuse de job.
There's no union in the factory.
You don't know English or French
                just a few words.
You think of Lisbon, the sonority of the language,
        the house poor but filled with sunshine,
        the fig trees in the garden.

You think too of Sacco and Vanzetti.
Here too you'll have to fight
and Immigrants don't have a lot of rights.

And the Immigrants in your homeland, do you know them?
In La Goutte d'Or, Aubervilliers, Nanterre
at the time of the Algerian war and the shanty towns.
Dirty nigger
Dirty Arab. France for the French.
Crowded into dormitories not fit for a dog.
Long lines at the police prefecture waiting for their
residency permit
which may not be renewed
eyes terrified—wanting a friendly word.
And the law on immigrants passed last summer practically
fascist. Yes, these countries are all alike.
Voiceless in Quebec.
You will not speak. Your voice mute, sealed. Look at the long
pink evenings on the birch, maple, and pine trees. Count the
stars in the early morning. Drink in this clean, crystalline, blue
light in the silence of the knifeblade nights. Curl up in waiting,
patience, the Rosinante of History will gallop again for you. You
will not speak. Small, humble, broken, immigrant words, birch
bark and samovar, like a distant lullaby plaintive and persistent,
piercing and pervasive, monotonous, stubborn. They rave, disrupt, explode.
They lose their bearings, their marbles.
They lose their tongue.
Memory cracked.
Memory split
the connections are screwed up.
There will be no narrative
no beginning, no middle, no end
no story.

Between she, I, and you all mixed up,
no order.
No chronology, no logic, no lodging.

France too
a colony.
The France of the little squares in the old quarters.
Streetcorners now gone
an apéro, a pastis, a calva on a zinc counter.
Today
    Crossroads
    Mammoth slashes prices
    Europe 1 is natural
    Put a tiger in your tank
    The France of the heights of Belleville
    The Paris of apartments at
        285,000 F: 50 sq. m., charming two-room
            apartment
        2,300,000 F: magnificent 180 sq. m. apartment
            on Île Saint-Louis
        375,000 F: beautiful two-room apartment
            in the 14th.
    France lost
        murdered
        with anti-Semitic graffiti on the walls of the métro.
    Don't cry it's all over
    schizophrenic city
        without hearth
        or home
    Nomadic space.

The letters connect, cavort, take flight, divide, come back together, encode themselves. Culture of the letter. Like autumn leaves blown away, piled up, rotting, abandoned. On the sloping roofs of the towns of Galicia, the moon still traces א, ב, ג, and ד;

in the gardens of the Ukraine, the stems of the sunflowers still form ש, ק, and ל; but no longer is there anyone to decode them, to grasp their meaning, their savour, their magic. Obligatory or forbidden letters, decorated letters of the scrolls of the Torah, handwritten. Sacred letters. An entire hidden wisdom is no longer revealed.

How would they have separated? How to end this story that isn't one? I don't know. One day she would have decided to leave. Mime Yente wouldn't even have tried to stop her. She would have taken an Air France 747 leaving from Mirabel at 20:45. Her books would follow by air freight and some furniture by boat in a container. She would have found herself back on Rue de la Mare in Paris, in the old neighbourhood of her childhood, her eyes full of new stars. She would have tried again to start over. She would have taken the métro again, line 10—Gare d'Orléans, Austerlitz, Porte d'Auteuil—without ever straying beyond Grenelle, dreaming of distant snows, of big low skies, of the Saint Lawrence locked in ice, of that quality of light she would never find again, of Mime Yente, and of her lost happiness.

Would there ever again be countries of lavender, summers, purple skies, warm nights? Nothing would ever again be as before. France would have changed.

> No order—no chronology, no logic, no lodging
> the connections are screwed up
> There will be no messiah,
> There will be no story
> just barely a plural voice
> a crossroads voice
> immigrant words.

II

Outremont

A story? I began: "I am neither knowledgeable nor ignorant. I have known some joys. That is saying too little." I recounted the whole thing, which they listened
to, it seemed to me, with interest, at least at the beginning. But the end was a surprise to both them and me.
"After that beginning," they said, "you will get to the
facts." How could I do that? The story was finished.

I had to admit that I was not capable of making a
story out of these events. I had lost the sense of narrative; it happens in many illnesses. But this explanation
only made them more demanding. I then noticed for
the first time that there were two of them, and that this
breach of the traditional method, although explained
by the fact that one was an eye specialist and the other
a specialist in mental illness, gave our conversation the
quality of an authoritarian interrogation under the sur-
veillance and control of a strict code. Granted, neither
one of them was the superintendent of police. But because they were two, they were three, and the third one
remained firmly convinced, I am sure, that a writer, a
man who speaks and who reasons with distinction, is
always capable of recounting the facts he remembers.

A story? No, not a story, never again.
—Maurice Blanchot, *La folie du jour*

Would one always have to start   All over again?
All over?
To leave again? Move again?
Another language   again?
In exile in one's own language.
The packsack always ready
for departure perhaps?
Immigrant words almost mute
                    without a shadow
                    without an echo
                    cracked
words from the stopping place before last.
Another part of the unending.

LINE 6—Nation to Étoile through Denfert-Rochereau. Nation before they built the express lines. The big demonstrations used to stop there. We'd climb the statue of Marianne in the middle of the square and plant red flags on her head and body. The school on Rue Marsoulan and the bakery where Anny bought milk rolls for her snack. PICPUS—BEL AIR—DAUMESNIL. The lions and the doctor's beautiful office. The waiting room looked like the set for an opera, with statues everywhere. That day, we'd put on our best clothes and best behaviour. BERCY—QUAI DE LA GARE. The métro crosses the Seine. Murky water, barges. It was raining. It rained often. It was always raining. Clanking of the old elevated métro. Anny liked the métro that —passes—in—the—day. The opposite bank. The other shore. Crossing the Seine or the Atlantic.

But I had tried. Another life, another neighbourhood, other social circles, a new adventure, this time among the Quebec bourgeoisie at the top of Outremont, in a beautiful house. Why this love of houses? Do I have to give her all my traits and all my passions? Did she experience the war, did she spend five years of her life moving almost every night, sleeping on the ground rolled in a blanket, panting with the fear of death in German words, German shouts. *Aufmachen! Raus! Schnell!* A house with a pine staircase as old as the illusion of rootedness.

THE DOOR CLOSES AGAIN, A COUNTRY

of one's own somewhere. Not strange. A place—a place—*heim,* a bed, indistinct on a shady street where no one would ever again come and put white crosses, marks, or seals. A house for dying a natural death in, of old age or sickness. She has to share something of this past. She must also live with this same dread.

The two-storey stone house would have a bay window in the front with a small round stained-glass window of delicate mauve. There would be three steps up to the front porch. There would be an oval foyer in inlaid wood, opening onto the living room on the street side and the dining room and kitchen in the back. The back yard would be filled with lilacs in spring. An old pine staircase, stripped, would lead to the second floor, to another oval area, brightened by a skylight, and the bedrooms and the bathroom, where in spring the light from the lilacs would cast purple reflections on the wall.

They would have put the piano, a beautiful Pleyel, in the foyer opposite the front door. The living room would be luxurious, with thick wool broadloom, covered by a Persian carpet forming a dark area in the centre. Under the lace-curtained bay window, a soft fawn-coloured couch from Roche-Bobois; on the right, a carved stone fireplace with an old iron grate. In an old bread bin from which the top had been removed, there would be a stereo system of the highest quality, and scattered around in no particular pattern, little walnut tables laden with art deco lamps and knick-knacks and ashtrays swiped from the Closerie des Lilas, often filled with Gauloise butts. She never would have changed her brand of cigarettes. On the walls, family photographs, lithographs, leather pieces worked by native people in faraway places, a Paris street sign, and mirrors. Everywhere, plants and vases of flowers. In the middle, an old pine rocker facing the fireplace, and a rustic little writing desk holding one of the household's telephones. The dining room would be more austere, containing only an oak table, six chairs, and a handsome pine china cabinet. They would have kept the original light fixture from the twenties, but a Tiffany lamp on a console table would sometimes provide more intimate lighting. Another Persian carpet would add to the warmth and cosiness of the room. On the wall, a large tapestry brought back from the Gaspé, and opposite it a set of curtained French doors opening directly onto a large back yard, snow-covered in winter, filled with roses and rhododendrons in summer. There would be another door to the garden from the kitchen, next to the dining room. The kitchen would be functional but with a Mexican touch from the pottery dishes and cookware filling every corner. On the upper floor, they would have made their bedroom in the large room over the living room, with the bay window and a balcony. Sunny in the morning, it would look like a page out of a decorating magazine. There would be a colourful quilt thrown on the bed, with all sorts of stuffed animals on it that she refused to part with. A sheepskin rug beside the bed would provide a contrast with the brightness of the quilt. A low walnut table near the window, and a large pine dresser with lots of drawers with white pulls, oval mirrors in delicate frames, and huge photographs of a part of old Paris. Pedestal tables of yew-wood would hold African statues acquired at auctions and big bouquets of flowers in vases from the Clignancourt flea market. The other room in the front would be a guest room, still almost empty, and in the back they would have their offices, perennially cluttered and filled with sunshine in the afternoon. The bathroom would be charmingly decorated with its little niches in the white wall holding hand towels, washcloths and bath mitts, health and beauty products, and pots of ivy climbing toward the light from the oval window. And larger niches holding books and magazines. It would be the perfect place for reading *Le Monde, Le Nouvel Observateur, Business Week, Fortune, Playboy,* and *Penthouse.* The bathtub and sink would be old-fashioned, with goose-neck faucets like the ones in American musical comedies. A rest room, but extravagant, a touch of the idyllic and pastoral for comfortable bourgeois. The basement would be a flight of stairs down from the oval foyer on the first floor. They wouldn't have finished it yet. For the time being, it would consist only of the furnace room and laundry room. The rest of the space would still be taken up by odds and ends they couldn't part with and big logs of birch and oak piled up to finish drying. At least three cords. The colour of the birch bark and the acrid smell of the still-damp wood would fill them with delight.

The large back yard would slope down toward Côte-Ste-Catherine, with a maple tree at the bottom. Shade all summer. Along the sides, rhododendrons, rose bushes, and masses of purple and blue irises. Nearer to the house, lilacs, lots of lilacs. They would have had to hire a gardener, it would cost a fortune, but still. What a beautiful garden! On the wall of the house facing the garden, the ivy would turn red in the fall, echoing the scarlet of the maple down the hill.

CHEVALERET. The Place d'Italie before they gutted the neighbourhood. The little bistrots around the square, the entrance to a store, Rue Bobillot where the little one used to go to do pottery, Thursdays I think it was. It was so long ago. The atelier was at the back of a courtyard. The Paris of the artisans still existed then and there were interior courtyards and low houses with crooked roofs. It was before the office towers and supermarkets. At the end of the courtyard there was a garden with mint and marjoram. You'd hear the machines of the tailor next door and a tinsmith a little further on. Life has gone on without them. CORVISART, GLACIÈRE. You had to get off at La Glacière and take Rue de la Glacière to the Reille intersection, and take Rue de la Colonie to the Place de l'Abbé-Hénocque. That square that was so quiet and shady was where they killed P. Goldmann—the memories of a Polish Jew born in France end there. A POLISH JEW MURDERED IN FRANCE. You remember the violent pain you felt when you heard the news. All around the square there were little old houses surrounded by gardens. One would feel at home in that house.

So I had imagined her in Outremont, marrying a lawyer or a psychiatrist, a professional anyway, who had become a deputy minister or senior civil servant and who spent a good part of the week in Quebec City but called her every day. I had imagined her trying to integrate into the Quebec bourgeoisie, with wrought iron fleurs de lys plastered all over her balcony. She would quickly have been hired by some literature or language department in a francophone university. She would have taught Soviet Jewish literature of the twenties, and she would have spent a long time on this poem by David Hofstein, which brought back her longing for the *shtetl,* her real country, which she would never have known:

> On Russian fields, in the twilights of winter!
> Where can one be lonelier, where can one be lonelier?
>
> The doddering horse, the squeaking sleigh,
> the path under snow—that is my way.
>
> Below, in a corner of the pale horizon,
> still dying, the stripes of a sad fallen sun.
>
> There, in the distance, a white wilderness,
> where houses lie scattered, ten or less,
> and—there—sleeps a shack, sunk deep in the snows.
>
> A house like the others—but larger, its windows . . .
> And in that house, to which many roads run,
> I am the eldest of all of the children. . . .
>
> And my world is narrow, my circle is small:
> in two weeks I've gone once into town—if at all.
>
> To long in the silence of space and of fields,
> of pathways and byways that snow has concealed. . . .
>
> To carry the hidden sorrowing
> of seeds that wait and wait for planting. . . .

On Russian fields, in the twilights of winter!
Where can one be lonelier, where can one be lonelier?

And her loneliness! But it's too soon. I have to go back. It wouldn't have been easy to get courses on Babel, Markish, Hofstein, but she finally would have done it, aided no doubt by the political circumstances. Wasn't she the wife of a senior civil servant? Didn't she have the required degrees? They would have given her the warmest welcome. A good job. No problem adjusting, good rapport, as they say, with students and with colleagues who tended to be touchy, new friends in journalism, politics, film, and publishing. She would spend a lot of time making herself attractive, caring for her body, feeling good about herself. She would go to the pool twice a week and get along well with the masseuse, whom she would always tip very well. I had given her some social causes to be active in, but nothing too extreme—human rights or legal aid or women's groups who were moderate in their tone and demands. Nothing subversive in the house near Côte-Ste-Catherine. Something humanitarian, accepted and even encouraged. She might perhaps even have headed a local branch of the group fighting for non-confessional schools, because she couldn't accept the remains of religiosity the Quiet Revolution had forgotten to sweep away. These remains would have proven tenacious, much more substantial than they seemed. Oh, come on! How could I imagine her in social democratic activities, her, the red with a Eurocommunist knife clutched in her teeth? Waiting for something better, no doubt, disoriented, tired, discouraged. With her new life, her new house, her beautiful garden. Waiting for the Godot of what Revolution? The Emma Bovary of politics. Waiting, waiting, for a left, a real one? She would have had to reassure Mime Yente, who would not have looked very kindly on this marriage to a goy, and who, being a great reader of *Commentary*, would have believed since November 15, 1976, that they were on the eve of a pogrom. Mime Yente

82

would have insisted on keeping Bilou, who, deprived of music, would have become melancholic. She would visit them in Snowdon once or twice a week. She would sit down at the piano. Bilou would immediately get up on top of the sheet music, curl up into a ball beside the metronome, and purr with pleasure. She would always bring a gift for Mime Yente, who would have taken up smoking a pipe and would befoul the whole house with her shag tobacco. They would have tea from the good old samovar from Zhitomir and Mime Yente would ask anxiously, "Nu, so what's new?"

She would always have to reassure her.

SAINT-JACQUES, where Michèle lived, across from La Santé prison. When she played the piano, they applauded. On Christmas night, they'd make a racket banging on pots. She had gotten used to hearing this racket once a year. Under the tracks of the elevated métro, the little old lady fed peanuts to thousands of pigeons.

In the summer they'd go to Paris. They would finally have bought the two-room apartment on Rue Mouffetard as a pied-à-terre in Paris. She would leave first, as soon as classes were over, and he would join her as soon as his activities at the ministry allowed. In winter they'd go to San Juan, Puerto Rico, or Barbados after the traditional Christmas visit to her in-laws in the Gaspé. They would eat the local tourtière—much better than the kind from Lac St-Jean—and go snowshoeing for hours. Everyone would be happy. She would have had to make them forget her too obvious "Frenchness," her accent with its imperceptible hint of cultural imperialism, her years at the Sorbonne and the École Normale Supérieure, her too perfect academic career, make them forget everything Parisian about her. She would generally do so quite easily, fascinated by this new horizon. So her husband would be a senior civil servant and would spend most of the week in Quebec City. She would have met him at a party at the home of friends in Outremont, a house very much like the one that would become hers, between two pastries and two glasses of wine. They would have talked about nothing at all at first, just exchanging banalities. "You're French, I see. How do you like it here? And the winter? Don't you miss Paris?" She would have questioned him about his work, about American psychiatry, and about psychoanalysis, that scourge Freud thought he had brought to the new world, which had quickly been transformed into a crutch, into valium.

They would not have spoken very much that evening. She wouldn't even have noticed that he had asked for her address and telephone number. A few days later, he would have called and invited her to dinner. Intrigued, she would have accepted rather automatically. He would have taken her to Les Halles on Crescent Street. She would have been extremely amused by this France out of an operetta, half René Clair, half American comedy. She would have found him attractive and teased him about his sober conservative dress and his accent. He would have laughed. He would have talked about himself at length, feeling comfortable with her. He would have gone to Collège Stanislas, then done medicine at the Université de Montréal and gone to the states to specialize. His father, a small industrialist from Trois-Rivières, would recently have died, leaving a widow and four sons. The widow would have gone back to the Gaspé after her husband's death. He'd be the eldest. He would have lost his religion—like everyone here—just before the Quiet Revolution, but his aged mother would continue to pray, and would have sulked over this French Jew with her old aunt who spoke only English and Yiddish—the last straw! But in the end it wouldn't have worked out too badly. The times would have changed; everyone would have become reconciled with otherness. For better or worse. Dreaming of an independent Quebec, he would have gotten involved in politics in the days of the RIN, belonging to the left wing. He would have supported the Parti Québécois from the beginning and even joined it later. He would have told her how he had been there in the square in front of the City Hall when de Gaulle spoke his famous "Vive le Québec libre!" How with thousands of others he had been overwhelmed, transported. How on November 15 they hadn't come down all night, happy, joyful, having regained a dignity that had for a long time been stifled, suppressed. She would have shared this profound joy, this new collective, communicative, healthy happiness. This feeling of finally existing, of belonging to a long lineage of struggles. They would have talked like this for a long time, feeling at home with each other. The meal would have been delicious. And that would have been how, between the poire belle-Hélène and the champagne, they decided never to part.

DENFERT-ROCHEREAU. The big lion and the huge intersection. It was mainly the transfer point for the Sceaux métro line, because at that time there were no express lines and to get to Fontenay-aux-Roses you had to go to Luxembourg or change at Denfert. Long grey platform, kiosk where you bought *Le Monde* and candy, long corridors full of people, with idiotic ads on the walls—"Parsley washes whiter" (they hadn't yet invented Mère Denis) or "Ya bon banania." In summer after it rained, it was so nice to walk on Rue Froideveaux in the smell of wet leaves.

RASPAIL. He lived on Rue Campagne-Première, in one of those beautiful, opulent bourgeois houses of the last century. His father was a commissioner of audit and he himself didn't know yet if he would study at the Conservatoire or have an important career in administration. You would get there early Saturday morning. He'd still be in bed, waiting for you, reading the previous night's *Le Monde* or *Le Nouvel Observateur*—I'm not sure if it was the *Nouvel Observateur* or the old *France Observateur*, it's so far away. You'd slip into bed beside him. The light in the room was the colour of spring lilacs. Nearing Raspail station, your heart would be beating hard. You were only eighteen. A long time after, taking the little one to the Centre Américain, you still remembered the feelings associated with the name Raspail, and later as a history teacher at the lycée, you could never speak of the old Republican without a quaver in your voice. They must have thought you really took your work seriously. Raspail. It's really only because of the colour of the curtains that you remember the light as being lilac.

Life would flow along, calm, easy. There would be roses in large vases of fine china, and a grand piano at the entrance of the oval foyer. She would spend hours at her piano playing old Hungarian melodies brought back from Budapest in days gone by, filled with longing for faraway places. Not for Paris, no. For great capitals with cacophonous, practically incomprehensible, indecipherable languages and long avenues where you could lose yourself and not be able to ask your way. Budapest and the Danube. The lovers on Margaret Island at the end of autumn. A cafeteria facing the Chain Bridge, and Janos who recited the poetry of Heine so beautifully. That would be far away, very far. She would most of all love walking in her neighbourhood, aimlessly, in any weather. It would always give her the same feeling of well-being. Especially in winter, on those windless evenings after a snowstorm, when the sky is very clear and all is silent. The sharply etched branches are bent with snow. The world shrinks. The lighted windows of the stone and brick houses shine, and in the clear night you can see fireplaces, old lamps, paintings, fine porcelain, antique guns, and knick-knacks. Beauty, wealth, security all around, the reassuring silence of a serene well-being. In the fall there were leaves crunching underfoot, gusts of wind, and the same transparent light that lets you participate in people's lives. She would walk for hours, especially in winter, after the snow, when the wind died down, loving the sharp, biting cold. She would spend hours at her piano.

Note all the differences. The old History textbooks.

7. Father Brébeuf and Father Lalement
Die with their Faithful

OBJECTIVE: To elicit admiration for the courage and un-
selfish charity of the early missionaries.

In the Land of the Indians

To make Canada a Catholic country, the missionaries went
to preach God's word to the various tribes. Among the
good Indians, the Black Robes succeeded in converting
several heathens from the same region, who then set up
small Christian villages. A missionary stayed among them,
said the Mass for them, administered the sacraments, and
continued to instruct them.

Among the bad Indians, the work was more difficult.
Often the Iroquois did not even want to see the Black
Robes. On the contrary, they intended to kill the mission-
aries and the Indian converts.

The Iroquois Attack

Father Brébeuf and Father Lalement worked with great
dedication in a Huron village. One night, war cries were
suddenly heard outside the palisade. It was the Iroquois
signal. They had come to put all the Christians to death.

Immediately, Father Brébeuf and Father Lalement ran
to get water and baptised all those who were ready for
baptism. Then they heard the confessions of all the adults.
They urged all the Christians to offer their lives to God for
the conversion of their enemies.

A hundred warriors were already running to defend
the palisade. They threw stones and shot arrows. But there
were a thousand Iroquois against them and they were not
able to force them to retreat. One after another the defend-
ers died under the blows of their adversaries.

Almost all the inhabitants of the village were massacred. Only Father Brébeuf and Father Lalement and a few

of their faithful were spared. They were taken prisoner so that they could be tortured.

The Christians are Taken to the Iroquois Village
On the way to the Iroquois village, the prisoners were beaten with sticks in the Iroquois manner. The Iroquois would line up on either side of a path, holding sticks, and strike the prisoners on the head and body as they went by. After passing through the whole group, the prisoners' bodies were completely covered with red and blue marks. In addition to this, their fingers were bitten and they were tortured in various other ways. The two missionaries did not think of their own sufferings. They comforted the Hurons and prayed for them. How brave they were to resist in this way!

When they got to the centre of the village, the prisoners were tied to stakes. Nearby, a big bonfire of branches was made. The Iroquois went from one prisoner to another, burning their flesh with flaming branches or pieces of red-hot iron.

The Fathers Comfort the Hurons
The missionary fathers knew how their companions would have to suffer. They repeated what they had taught them in the catechism: "Bear your sufferings with courage and look up to heaven, your eternal reward. The torments of earth will not last long, but the reward God gives to those who are faithful to Him endures forever."

The Hurons admired the courage and charity of the missionaries and drew comfort from their words. They promised to remain faithful and to pray to God until their last breath.

The missionaries could have no greater joy than to see these new converts praying in preparation for their martyrdom. They knew their faithful Christians would soon be in Heaven.

The cruel Iroquois, inspired by the devil, invented the most terrible ways of making their victims suffer! They saved the must painful tortures for the Black Robes. One after another, they pierced their skin with red-hot iron rods. They pulled out their fingernails. They put hot coals on their wounds. The missionaries only prayed to God for the courage to bear so much pain.

The Martyrdom of Father Brébeuf

The Indians strung some tomahawk blades together and heated them in the fire until they were red-hot. Then they put them around Father Brébeuf's neck like a necklace. Despite his sufferings, Father Brébeuf continued to offer encouragement to his companions. In his strong voice, he spoke about Jesus Christ. It enraged the Iroquois to hear him. Becoming even more brutal, they scalped him and poured hot ashes on his head. The Iroquois were furious to see him resist their tortures for so long.

Of all the tortures, the Iroquois seemed to prefer that of fire. They went into the forest and removed the bark from some pine trees. They put it all around the body of Father Brébeuf and lighted it. All his flesh was burned and blackened.

The martyr was still breathing, expecting death at any moment. His executioners were surprised to see so much courage in a man. Then one of them decided to finish him off. He struck the missionary on the left side with his tomahawk, opening his chest, and tore out his heart and ate it.

Generous Father Brébeuf will be rewarded in Heaven for his work and his sacrifices.

The Martyrdom of Father Lalement

Father Lalement endured similar torture by the Iroquois. They traced a cross on his thigh and put a red-hot tomahawk in the wound. However the father did not stop praying for the Hurons who were dying around him. He could no longer speak because they had burned his throat, but he could still turn his eyes to heaven where he hoped soon to go. The murderers could not tolerate this gesture. They tore out his eyes and put hot coals in their place.

Father Lalement suffered the most horrible torments for more than fifteen hours. His whole body was one wound from head to foot. To finish him off, a warrior struck him on the head with a tomahawk, opening his skull.

He too was rewarded for his martyrdom. God accepted the sufferings of the martyrs. He allowed Catholicism to thrive in our country.

Martyrs of Today

Father Brébeuf and Father Lalement are among our blessed Canadian martyrs. They are models of heroism for today's missionaries who are persecuted by the wicked. The good Lord still chooses His martyrs in foreign missions. Priests, religious, and ordinary Christians must endure much suffering in some countries. They are forbidden to speak of the Lord. They are even put to death because they want to let all men know about Jesus Christ and to practise their religion openly.

Following the example of our holy Canadian martyrs, they show great strength under persecution. One day God will reward their sacrifices. Let us with our prayers help them remain faithful unto death.

SAINT JEAN DE BRÉBEUF,
PRAY FOR US!
SAINT GABRIEL LALEMENT,
PRAY FOR US!

✝

Boulevard Edgar-Quinet along the Cimetière du Montparnasse. Chez Mimile. In those days, we spent hours at Chez Mimile. No one was in a rush. They weren't after maximum profit. A golden light filled the old-fashioned bistrot with its ceil-

ing mouldings and shaded light fixtures. There were white laven-
der-scented tablecloths on the tables and prints on the walls in a
naive style imitating ex-votos. You remember their pintade au
chou and tarte Tatin. Chez Mimile was a find. He moved, driven
out by the speculators who've renovated the whole neighbourhood. Another bit of old Paris that's gone. Chez Mimile had an
old, badly tuned piano at the back of the room. After a meal
you'd often sit down at it and play old ballads of yesteryear, imitating a barrel organ. The customers seemed to like it, and asked
for more. One day Mimile asked you to come play on a Saturday
night. For that occasion, there was a vase with a rose in it on each
table. You played some syrupy tunes from the thirties, softly so as
not to hinder conversation but still loudly enough to make the
clients feel the mood, somewhat in the style of the Closerie des
Lilas after the war.

AFTER GRENELLE
      I DON'T KNOW ANY MORE
THE LINE GETS LOST IN MY
      MEMORY
THE OPERATION   WAS CALLED
    SPRING   WIND
AFTER   GRENELLE

Note all the differences, give body and shape to the differences. Especially the advertising for Ben's:

Here are some of our world-famous specialties . . .

    Hot smoked meat sandwich

    Golden brown potato latkes

    Smoked meat fried rice

    Ben's oriental delicacy

    Two smoked meat egg rolls with plum sauce

    BIG BENS SANDWICH

    Bens famous hot smoked meat served on double rye

    bread with pickle, cole slaw, and French fries.

Hot cheese blintzes with rich sour cream, apple sauce or blueberry sauce.

Rib steak, filet mignon, brochette

SPAGHETTI À LA BENS

With chopped hot Bens smoked meat and rich meat sauce

HOLL-IPP-CHIS DELIGHT

Two stuffed cabbage rolls in sauce, potatoes and la Parisienne Broit.

Cheesecake freshly baked on our premises

Tarte à la mode pie

Buvez le Bens special glacé ice cold

Breuvages à la fontaine

Fountain drinks

COUNTER OR TABLE SERVICE

DELICATESSEN FOODS TO TAKE OUT

BENS IS OPEN FROM 7 A.M. TO 4 A.M. (SUNDAY THROUGH THURSDAY) AND 7 A.M. TO 5 A.M. (FRIDAY AND SATURDAY).

BENS—A FAMILY BUSINESS SINCE 1908.

BENS a Montreal tradition.

The evolution of Bens Restaurant-Delicatessen from its meager beginnings in 1908 would have made a terrific screenplay for a Hollywood movie. It's the story of a 16 year old boy, Ben Kravitz, who left the oppression of Europe for the hope and freedom of the New World. Upon his arrival in Canada in 1899, Ben's only assets were a passion for hard work, a great sympathy for human beings and the recipe for Ben's Smoked Meat.

Ben settled in Montreal, and in 1904 married his wife, Fanny, forming the lifelong partnership that would eventually produce four children, Sol, Al, Irving and Gertrude, and a successful family restaurant business.

In 1908, Fanny decided to open a small shop in Montreal's garment district selling canned goods, fruits and biscuits. Ben noticed that when the factory girls visited the store they asked for sandwiches. Remembering back to his youth in Lithuania where his grandfather used to pickle smoked beef briskets, Ben saw an opportunity to satisfy this demand by preparing smoked beef and serving it as a sandwich.

At first, there was resistance to his strange looking meat sandwich. However, word soon spread throughout the garment district about this wonderful delicacy, and Bens smoked meat sandwiches captured a loyal following.

At the onset of the Depression, the family took on its greatest gamble. The business was moved into the heart of Montreal's hotel/tourist district, to the corner of Boulevard de Maisonneuve and Metcalfe. At the same time, the name was changed to Bens De Luxe Delicatessen-Sandwich Shop. It was this gamble that resulted in the present prosperity and international renown of Bens.

As demand for Bens products grew, so did the need for an even larger store. In 1949, Ben opened a new restaurant across the street and kept the old store in operation to satisfy the overflow capacity.

Since 1908, Bens has become a Montreal landmark. Celebrities as far away as California eat air-expressed Bens Sandwiches, while over 500,000 customers a year eat at the restaurant. Today the business continues to be operated by the Kravitz family—and while the world has changed since 1908, the family maintains the same high standards as established by Mr. Ben.

But sometimes the anxiety, as if what had been excluded was stealing in at the very place of the lack, the very place of the absence, as if what was excluded could start gnawing at her day after day. Like a rising wave, at first distant, muted, indistinct, then stronger and stronger. Scraps, fragments of conversations, of meetings, of assemblies. Rumblings of large crowds, demonstrations, slogans, songs, banners, bits of meetings in school gyms on the eve of municipal, legislative, cantonal, or presidential elections or referendums—pieces of History stratified and crumbling. Rumblings that would be familiar to her from having taken part in the marches, the shouting, sharing their calendar, their everyday space, their breathing for so many years. With no order, logical or chronological. No to fascism! Pompidou—we want ours too! Victory to the NLF! USA go home! Peace in Algeria! VIVE—LE—FLN! Barre one—Barre two—Bar you! Discard Giscard! They soon shall hear the bullets flying, we'll shoot the generals on our own side. 'Tis the final conflict. Allons enfants de la patrie. Unity in action! El pueblo unido nunca será vencido. Chile will overcome! Pinochet murderer! Cuba si, Yankee no! Cuba si, Yankee no! Che Che Che! Hands off Chile! Racists—fascists—murderers! We are all German Jews! Immigrant workers, French workers—one boss, one struggle! The bosses' goons—fascists—killers! CFT sellouts! Make the bosses pay! Schools, not guns! Funding! Long live May 1st! Unity—Unity! Shouting, clamour, tears, clenched fists, protests, our solidarity, often our powerlessness. People of the world, circle the world, circle the world with peace. Peace in Algeria! Peace in Vietnam! USA murderers! Long live the Tet offensive! Free Ritsos, free Theodorakis! Save Grimau. Franco murderer! Venceremos! PIDE murderers! SAVAK murderers! No arms for apartheid! Bold ideas sharpened like knives. Only one answer—a common program! One solution—revolution! CRS = SS! OAS murderers! Avanti popolo, alla riscossa, bandiera rossa, bandiera rossa. Avanti popolo alla riscossa, bandiera rossa trionferà. Old wounds or joys, old battles won or lost. The fabric of everyday life unravelled. Vote no! No to dictatorship! No to Badinguet! No to de Gaulle! No to the authoritarian constitution! No to article 16! No to special powers! No to Ridgway! No to Jules Moch and his tanks! No to a German Europe! No to the CED! Peace in Indo-China! Free Henri Martin! No to German rearmament! A forty-hour week! The state, the bosses—one enemy! The state cuts, the law cheats! Arise, ye prisoners of starvation. No saviour from on high delivers. Long live the FLN! Free our comrades! Barre—Barre—bullshitter! Ten years is enough! It's flying, it's moving forward, it's the workers' flag. Students and workers—solidarity! Down with the Laniel decrees! Bon voyage, Monsieur Guy Mollet! Long live July 14! At the call of the great Lenin, the partisans rose up. De Gaulle, Pohier, no difference! Respect the Oder-Neisse line! Long live the Commune! 'Tis the final conflict. Arise, ye prisoners of starvation. We will not forget. We will not allow. We will avenge you, we will punish the murderers. You did not die in vain. Solidarity forever. History will decide, History the final judge. Long live July 14! There are other Bastilles to be stormed! The people of Paris. The streets of Paris. Gavroche and Liberty Guiding the People. Let's march in step, comrades, let's march bravely forward together. Beyond the barricades, freedom awaits. Retirement at sixty! No funding for religious schools. Down with the church! Down with censorship! Power is in the street! Unlimited general strike. Charlie, money! Don't give up, keep up the fight! Charonne—shame on the police! Honey, listen to the whistles of the factories and the trains in the city. Everyone to La Mutu! Everyone to Père Lachaise. Everyone to the Élysée. Power to the workers! From La République to La Bastille by way of Boulevard Voltaire, from La Nation to La Bastille by way of Faubourg Saint-Antoine or Boulevard Beaumarchais. It was nice out. It was cold. It was raining. There were hardly any people. There were lots of people. A million according to *L'Huma,* two hundred thousand according to the prefecture of police, five hundred thousand according to *Le Monde.* It was a great demo. I've just come back from the demo. Everyone to the demo! No saviour from on high delivers, No faith have we in prince or peer!

This practice of the ordinary, this politics of everyday, now left behind, would assail her, shouting in her ears the slogans from events that would from now on be separate from her. Cut off from her History, thrown into another. Lack. Could hope be the same the world over, and would she ever be able to find herself in it? Without the shared itineraries and voices, without that secular fabric of codes of thought and action, of reflexes? Here the workers' day is not May 1st, it's the first Monday in September. She wouldn't be able to get used to it. She'd never get over it. Why all this anxiety and this massive intrusion of the political, since I insist on putting her in a bourgeois setting? The better to mix things up. But what things? She would have established her own analogies, references, events with which she could identify here. Struggles she would understand, a common language. Something vaguely universal that would allow her not to feel the dismemberment. A mixed catalogue, a vade-mecum for left-wing exiles. A huge packsack containing, willy-nilly, not in chronological order, first, the f manifesto. That would ring like the old echo of a national liberation struggle, something she would have been altogether familiar with. Her husband would often have described the intense emotion that had gripped him when he heard it read by Gaston Montreuil on Radio-Canada.

> The Front de Libération du Québec is not the Messiah or a modern-day Robin Hood. It is a group of Quebec workers who have decided to do what is necessary in order that the Quebec people may once and for all take control of its destiny.
>
> The Front de Libération du Québec wants complete independence for the Québécois, united in a free society purged forever of its clique of voracious sharks, the bosses and their valets who have made Quebec their private preserve of cheap labour for unscrupulous exploitation.
>
> The Front de Libération du Québec is not a violent movement but a response to violence, the violence organized by high finance with its puppets, the federal and provincial governments (the Brinks show, Bill 63, the electoral map, the so-called social progress tax, Power Corporation, doctors' insurance, the Lapalme boys, etc.).

The Front de Libération du Québec finances itself through "voluntary taxes" collected from companies who exploit the workers (banks, finance companies, etc.).

"The rich and powerful of the status quo, most of them the traditional guardians of our people, have obtained the response they wanted, retreat, rather than the change for which we have worked as never before and for which we will keep on working." (René Lévesque, April 29, 1970)

The "Democracy" of the Rich

For a while we thought channelling our energy and our impatience, as René Lévesque put it so well, into the Parti Québécois, would be effective, but the Liberal win shows very well that what is called democracy in Quebec is in fact and always has been "democracy" only for the rich. The Liberal Party win is only a victory of the Simard-Cotroni electoral machine. British parliamentary government is finished, and the Front de Liberation du Québec will never allow itself to be distracted by the electoral crumbs the Anglo-Saxon capitalists throw into the animal pen of Quebec every four years. Many Québécois have understood this and they are going to take action. In the coming year, Bourassa will grow up: there will be 100,000 organized and armed revolutionary workers!

Yes, there are reasons for the Liberal win. Yes, there are reasons for poverty, unemployment, slums, for the fact that you, Monsieur Bergeron on Rue Visitation, and you, Monsieur Legendre in Laval, who earn $10,000 a year, do not feel free in our country of Quebec.

Yes, there are reasons, and the guys from Lord know them, and the fishermen in the Gaspé, the workers on the North Shore, and the miners at Iron Ore, Quebec Cartier Mining, and Noranda also know the reasons. And the decent workers at Cabano who they tried to screw yet again know a whole lot of reasons.

"Golden Vessels"

Yes, there are reasons why you, Monsieur Tremblay on
Rue Panet, and you, Monsieur Cloutier who works in
construction in St-Jérôme, why you can't buy yourselves
"golden vessels" with all kinds of fancy doodads like
Drapeau the aristocrat did, who's so concerned about
the slums that he had coloured panels put up in front of
them so that the rich tourists wouldn't see our misery.

Yes, there are reasons why you, Madame Lemay in
St-Hyacinthe, can't afford to take little trips to Florida
like the crooked judges and politicians do with our
money.

The decent workers of Vickers and Davie Ship who
were sacked without being given any reason, they know
the reasons. And the guys from Murdochville who were
punished just for wanting to unionize, who the crooked
judges forced to pay over two million dollars for wanting
to exercise this basic right, they know justice and they
know a lot of reasons.

Yes, Monsieur Lachance on Rue Ste-Marguerite,
there are reasons why you drown your despair, your
bitterness, your rage in Molson's cheap beer. And you,
Lachance junior, with your marijuana cigarettes . . .

A Lot of Reasons

Yes, there are reasons why you welfare recipients are
kept on the dole from generation to generation. There
are a lot of reasons, and the Domtar workers in Windsor
and East Angus know them. And the Squibb and Ayers
workers and the guys at the Liquor Board and 7-Up and
Victoria Precision, and the blue-collar workers in Laval
and Montreal and the Lapalme boys know a lot of
reasons.

The Dupont of Canada workers know them too, even
though they will soon only be able to give them in English
(assimilated, they'll swell the ranks of the immigrants,
the new Quebeckers, the favoured children of Bill 63).

And the Montreal police, who are the fist of the system, should also have understood the reasons; they should have realized that we live in a terrorized society, because without their force, without their violence, nothing worked on October 7!

"Canadian" Federalism

We've had it with the Canadian federalism that penalizes Quebec milk producers in order to satisfy the needs of the Anglo-Saxons of the Commonwealth; that keeps the decent taxi drivers of Montreal in a state of semi-slavery while shamefully protecting the exclusive monopoly of the disgusting Murray Hill and its murderer owner Charles Hershorn and his son Paul, who several times on the evening of October 7 grabbed a twelve-calibre rifle from his employee's hands to fire on the drivers and fatally wounded Corporal Dumas, who was killed as a demonstrator; whose stupid trade policy throws small wage-earners in textiles and shoes, the most abused in Quebec, out on the street one by one for the profit of a handful of goddamn moneymakers in Cadillacs; that puts the Quebec nation among the ethnic minorities of Canada.

We've had it, and so have more and more Québécois, with a gutless government that does a thousand and one cartwheels to beg the American millionaires to invest in Quebec, La Belle Province, where thousands of square miles of forests full of game and lakes full of fish are the exclusive property of these same all-powerful Lords of the twentieth century;

The Brinks Armoured Cars

with a hypocrite like Bourassa, who uses Brinks' armoured cars, a true symbol of the foreign occupation of Quebec, to keep the poor Québécois "natives" in fear of the misery and unemployment we have become so accustomed to;

with our taxes that the Ottawa envoy to Quebec wants to give to the anglophone bosses to "encourage" them, my dear, to speak French, to negotiate in French; repeat after me, "main-d'oeuvre à bon marché means cheap labour";

with promises of jobs and prosperity, because we will always be the diligent servants and bootlickers of the big shots as long as there are Westmounts, Town of Mount Royals, Hampsteads, Outremonts, the strongholds of high finance of Saint James Street and Wall Street, as long as all of us Québécois do not put them out by whatever means, including dynamite and arms, those bosses of the economy and politics who stoop to anything to screw us.

We live in a society of terrorized slaves, terrorized by the big bosses, Steinberg, Clark, Bronfman, Smith, Neopole, Timmins, Geoffrion, J.-L. Lévesque, Hershorn, Thompson, Nesbitt, Desmarais, Kierans (beside them, Rémi Popol the bludgeon, Drapeau the dog, Bourassa the Simards' dummy, and Trudeau the fag are peanuts!).

The Great Masters of Consumption
Terrorized by the Roman Capitalist Church, even if it is less and less obvious (who owns the Place de la Bourse?), by loan repayments to Household Finance, by the advertising of the great masters of consumption, Eaton, Simpson, Morgan, Steinberg, General Motors, etc.; terrorized by the closed doors of learning and culture that are the universities, and by their monkey principals Gaudry and Dorais and the sub-monkey Robert Shaw.

More and more of us are coming to know and suffer this terrorist society and the day is coming when all the Westmounts will disappear from the map of Quebec.

Production, mining, and forestry workers, service workers, teachers and students, unemployed workers, take what is yours, your work, your determination, and your freedom. And you, General Electric workers, you're the ones who keep your factories going; only you are able to produce; without you, General Electric is nothing!

Workers of Quebec, start today taking back what belongs to you; take for yourselves what is yours. Only you know your factories, your machines, your hotels, your universities, your trade unions. Don't wait for a miracle organization.

Make Your Revolution
Make your revolution yourselves in your neighbourhoods, in your workplaces. If you don't do it yourselves, technocrats or other usurpers will replace the little group of cigar smokers we have now and we'll have to start all over again. You alone are capable of building a free society.

We must struggle, no longer one by one but united until victory, with all the means in our possession, as the Patriotes of 1837-38 did (who our Holy Mother the Church rushed to excommunicate, the better to sell out to British interests).

In the four corners of Quebec, let those they have dared call lousy French and alcoholics vigorously take up the battle against the destroyers of freedom and justice and put out of commission all those professional hold-up artists and swindlers: bankers, businessmen, judges, and sell-out political wheeler-dealers.

We are Québécois workers and we will go to the limit. We want to replace this entire society of slaves with a free society that functions by itself and for itself, a society open to the world.

Our struggle can only end in victory. An awakened people cannot long be held in misery and contempt.

Vive le Québec libre!
Long live our comrades, the political prisoners!
Long live the Quebec revolution!
Long live the Front de Libération du Québec!

1970

She would often wonder how she herself would have reacted to these events. Wouldn't she have called the FLQ petty-bourgeois populists cut off from the people? Idealistic dreamers playing with fire? Would she have been won over? Would she too have felt that emotion on hearing their message? At several years remove, this text would sound strangely close and strangely distant.

There would also be in that heavy packsack, in that timeless puzzle she would have put together day after day, the declaration of independence of February 28, 1838, which featured equal rights for the native peoples, separation of church and state, the abolition of fiefdoms, freedom of the press, etc. She would readily identify with it. All in all, a bourgeois revolution a little bit late. Good for the packsack. Searching in the bag, you'd find the whole trade union movement and the landmark strikes, especially Murdochville. Her husband, being a Gaspésien, would often have spoken of that little company town of three thousand people in the fifties. A seven-month struggle against Noranda Mines. A thousand workers. It was a crime to affiliate with the steelworkers of the CIO. The Labour Relations Board set up by the villainous Duplessis had refused them accreditation in spite of the fact that they had a clear majority. Noranda instigated a company union. In 1956, the Steelworkers' Union, under the leadership of Émile Boudreau, got eight hundred cards signed and filed an application for accreditation. On March 8, 1957, Théo Gagné, the president of the union local, was suddenly fired. The union responded with a long strike. Defeated. Yes, this would have been one of her battles, she would identify fully with it, as if she had been there herself in the fifties, newly arrived in Canada, the wife of a miner, fighting fiercely from the depths of *la grande noirceur* against the company unions, the trumped-up commissions serving the powerful, the blacklists, the Padlock Law, the starvation wages, and the clergy, the repression in all its forms. The Dominion Textile strike of 1946 in Valleyfield as well, and Kent Rowley telling the court that he was there as a result of a conspiracy between Duplessis and Dominion Textile, and Madeleine Parent and Bernard Mergler defending the trade unionists. Yes, all that would be her world, her lifelong values. The union movement that refused to take orders, that rejected anticommunism and the law of the carrot and the stick. But that would still not be enough for her. Searching the packsack, you'd also find the struggle to build a left here, Fred Rose and the manifestoes of Parti Pris and the PSQ, the MLP, the FLP, and FRAP, and the debate on reformism, and that workers' party always to be built and never built. There again, she would identify fully, not feeling at all strange. There would simply be a big hole where at home what was called the Socialist or Communist Party was, that was all. A huge hole—an absence that was horribly present, painful, an enormous emptiness that would crush her at the first opportunity. In her packsack of identifications, there would also be women, their quest, their struggle, their writing. The women against the incredible reactionary stupidity that had censored *Les fées ont soif*. Women like Yolande Tanguay, a miner's daughter married to a miner from Thetford Mines, who wanted "to show that the important people in town aren't the only ones who have something to say. A worker can speak just as well as anyone else. They say speech is the vehicle of thought. Let's try to make sure it's not an old jalopy. I have a souped-up dune buggy and I wouldn't want a Cadillac. Let's try to express ourselves in our own language and we'll get to our destination somehow. Who wants to come along in my souped-up dune buggy?" In the packsack would also be all the agit-prop and recent literature and art of this country, from Borduas to Hubert Aquin. The first real pain she had felt here was at the suicide of Aquin. And then the inevitable aftermath: his name given to a building of the Université du Québec. The man who had died would have been horrified by that. Yes, the writing from here, in which she would have immersed herself from the first day. On the side of those who struggled. And what about the national question, Madame?

Note all the differences. Do not forget Bernard Derome tonight on the news. The television programs:

❷ CBFT

8.55 Ouverture et horaire
9.00 En mouvement
9.15 Les 100 tours de Centour
9.30 Animagerie
10.00 Passe-partout
10.30 Magazine-express
« La chiropratique » avec le Dr Roch Parent, chiropraticien. « Soins dentaires » avec le Dr Yves Dufresne, chirurgien-dentiste
11.00 Moi aussi je parle français : « La Beauce ». Le français parlé dans la Beauce, ce « québécois provincial », tient ces particularités de nombreuses influences : amérindienne, acadienne, irlandaise, etc., aussi bien que de l'imagerie populaire.
11.30 Gaspard et les fantômes : Dessins animés
12.00 Un pays, un gout, une manière : Documentaire réalisé par Iolande Cadrin-Rossignol et Fernand Dansereau. « La lecon du passé »
12.30 Les coqueluches : Inv. : Danièle Doris et Clairette
13.30 Le téléjournal
13.35 Femme d'aujourd'hui : « Les femmes de Montréal sont-elles différentes des femmes de Québec ? Les hommes anglophones voient-ils les femmes autrement que les hommes francophones ? » Il y a moyen de le savoir et d'en apprendre bien plus encore sur ce que nous sommes.
14.30 Les ateliers
15.30 Les animaux chez eux : « Au pays des serpents a sonnettes ».
16.00 Bobino
16.30 Les héritiers
17.00 Le coeur au ventre. Feuilleton réalisé par Robert Mazoyer
18.00 Ce soir
19.00 Propulsion CTF
19.30 Génies en herbe : Jeu-questionnaire
20.00 Frédéric : Téléroman de Michel Faure et Claude Fournier.
20.30 Hors-série : « Gaston Phébus » (Le lion des Pyrénées). D'après l'oeuvre de Myriam et Gaston de Béarn. Avec Jean-Claude Drouot, Pascale Rivault, Georges Marchal, Dora Doll et Michèle Grellier.
21.30 Consommateurs plus : « Les dessous d'une vente ». Les ventes que nous annoncent les magasins sont-elles véritables ? A qui profitent-elles ? Fait-on un bon achat ? « La loi 72 » nouvelle loi de protection du consommateur entrera en vigueur au mois de mars. Les éléments les plus importants seront analysés.
22.00 L'enjeu. Anim. : Gilles Courtemanche. Interviews, tables rondes et sondages concernant la question référendaire.
22.30 Le téléjournal
23.10 Nouvelles du sport
23.20 Cinéma : « Le bon et le méchant » (français 1975). Comédie réalisé par Claude Lelouch, avec Jacques Dutronc, Marlène Jobert, Bruno Cremer, Jacques Villeret et Brigitte Fossey.
1.30 Ciné-nuit : « Sangaree » (américain 1952). Drame réalisé par Edward Ludwig, avec Fernando Lamas, Arlene Dahl et Patricia Medina...
3.05 Le téléjournal

❿ CFTM

6.55 Horaire
7.00 Les p'tits bonshommes
8.00 Gronico et Cie
8.30 Le 10 vous informe
8.35 Bonjour le monde. Avec Michel Jasmin.
10.00 Votre amie Suzanne : « De belles choses », « La famille et ses droits », « La décoration intérieure »
11.15 Saturnin, le petit canard
11.30 Le 10 vous informe
12.30 Ciné-quiz : « La justice du pendu » (américain 1974). Western avec Steve Forrest, Dean Jagger, Will Geer et Sharon Acker.
14.30 Jeannette veut savoir : « S'il faut donner la fessée a un enfant »

15.30 Les services a la communauté
16.00 Les satellipopettes
16.30 Ma sorcière bien-aimée
17.00 Patrouille du cosmos
18.00 Le 10 vous informe
18.30 Les Tannants
19.30 Féminin pluriel
20.00 Réferendum: Anim.: Jacques Morency
21.00 Bonsoir le monde. Avec Michel Jasmin
22.00 Toute la ville en parle
22.15 La corne d'abondance
22.30 Sport au 10
23.10 La couleur du temps
23.25 Programme double: « La violence appelle l'ordre » (italien 1973). Drame policier réalisé par Sergio Martino, avec Luc Merenda, Richard Conte, Silvanio Tranquill, Martine Borchard, Carlo Alighlero et Cristea Avram.
 1.00 Programme double: « Nuit d'or » (franco-allemand 1976) — Drame de moeurs réalisé par Serge Moati, avec Klaus Kinski, Anny Duperey et Valérie Pascale.
 2.30 Dernière édition

⑰ RADIO-QUEBEC
10.00 Le marché aux images. Films documentaires.
11.00 Readalong. Child Life in Other Lands. Émission du ministère de l'Éducation destinée a favoriser l'apprentissage de la langue anglaise chez les jeunes.
11.30 Parlez-moi. Avec l'ami Sol, les jeunes anglophones apprennent le français.
13.30 Mon ami Pierrot
13.45 Les 100 tours de Centour
14.00 Passe-partout. Une émission divertissante pour les petits de trois a six ans.
14.30 Le marché aux images. Films documentaires.
15.30 La vie en mouvement: « La vie des libellules »
16.00 Le mime Marcel Marceau
17.00 La houille verte. Un document sur le phénomène de photosynthèse.
17.30 Métrique. Les secrets du système métrique.

18.00 Le petit monde d'André Tahon
18.30 C'est arrivé a Hollywood: « Les mondes imaginaires ». Série d'émissions faisant revivre les meilleurs moments du cinéma hollywoodien.
19.00 La vie parlementaire
20.00 Babillart. Un magazine culturel qui nous fait connaître artistes et créateurs de chez nous.
20.30 Cinq milliards d'hommes: « L'échange inégal ». Le phénomène de détérioration des échanges entre les pays.
21.00 Les livres et nous. Un rendez-vous avec le monde de l'écriture québécoise.
21.30 I am the Blues. Willie Dixon et ses musiciens nous font partager quelques moments de leur existence et de leur passion, le blues.

⑨⑨ TVFQ (Câble)
 9.30 Pour les jeunes: « Hebdo jeune »: « Modelisme: visite du Club Boulogne Billancourt ».
10.15 Feuilleton: « Une femme seule » d'après le roman de Régine Andry. Avec Dominique Vilar.
10.30 Société d'aujourd'hui. Inv.: Dr Jean-Paul Escande, Dr Gilbert Tordjmann, Rose Codina, Gaelle Questiaux. Rubrique d'information médicale, de conseils de beauté et de mode.
11.30 Midi-Première: Variété
12.00 A la découverte de...
13.00 Au théâtre ce soir. « Le faiseur » d'Honoré de Balzac avec Jean Le Poulain, Francoise Fleury, Martine Couture et Jean-Marie Bernicat.
15.00 Des chiffres et des lettres.
15.20 Passez donc chez moi
15.40 Actualités régionales: L'est de la France
17.00 Pour les jeunes: « Hebdo jeune »
17.45 Feuilleton: « Une femme seule » d'après le roman de de Régine Andry. Avec Dominique Vilar.
18.00 Société d'aujourd'hui. Cinq candidats, tous auteurs-compositeurs-interprètes, tentent leur chance devant un jury de téléspectatrices présidé par deux personnalités du spectacle.

19.00 Midi-Première: Variété
19.30 A la découverte de...: «Avant Marseille». Il y a 2 500 ans, Marseille était une cité grecque dont le développement n'a pas cessé depuis cette époque.
20.30 Au théâtre ce soir. «Ne quittez pas». Comédie en deux actes et trois tableaux de Marc-Gilbert Sauvajon et Guy Bolton sur une idée d'Albert Savoir. Avec Jean-Pierre Bouvier, Mario Game, Jose Luccioni et Henri Courseaux.
22.30 Des chiffres et des lettres
23.00 Passez donc chez moi
23.10 Actualités régionales: L'est de la France

🄶 CBMT
9.00 A Thought for Today
9.05 CBC 6 Good Morning
9.15 The Friendly Giant
9.30 Quebec School Telecast
10.00 Canadian Schools
10.30 Mr. Dressup
11.00 Sesame Street
11.58 Weather Report
12.00 From Now On
12.28 Senior Citizens' Bulletin Board
12.38 Wicks
13.00 Today from the Pacific
14.00 The Edge of Night
14.30 Take 30
15.00 The Bob McLean Show
16.00 Beyond Reason
16.30 All in the Family
17.00 The Beachcombers
17.30 The Mary Tyler Moore Show
18.00 The City at Six
19.00 Happy Days
19.30 Nellie, Daniel, Emma and Ben
20.00 Archie Bunker's Place
20.30 Front Page Challenge
21.00 The Tommy Hunter Show
22.00 Dallas
23.00 The National

23.27 The City Tonight
23.45 Brier Reports
24.00 All That Jazz
1.00 Cine-Six. «Love is a Ball» (comédie 1963) avec Glenn Ford, Hope Lange, Charles Boyer, Ricardo Montalban et Telly Savalas.
2.55 Station closing

🄻🄴 CFCF
5.59 Sign on
6.00 University of the Air
6.30 Morning Exercises
7.00 Canada A.M.
9.00 Romper Room
9.30 What's Cooking
10.00 Ed Allen
10.30 Definition
11.00 The Community
11.30 Rocket Robin Hood
12.00 The Flintstones
12.30 Street Talk
13.00 McGowan and Co.
13.30 The Allan Hamel Show
14.30 Another World
16.00 The Mad Dash
16.30 Family Feud
17.00 The Price Is Right
18.00 Pulse
19.00 McGowan and Co.
19.30 Grand Old Country
20.00 The Love Boat
21.00 The Dukes of Hazzard
22.00 The Olympiad: The Marathon
22.58 Loto-Québec
23.00 CTV National News
23.21 Pulse
24.00 Twelve Midnight Movie: «Claudine» (comédie dramatique 1974) avec Diahann Carroll et James Earl Jones.
1.45 «Climb an Angry Mountain» (Drame 1972) avec Fess Parker, Arthur Hunicutt et Marg Dusay.
3.35 Sign off

They would sometimes have painful discussions that were close to quarrels. When the government passed a special law suspending the right to strike, she would have made sarcastic comments on its "prejudice in favour of the workers." He would have raised his voice. He would have gotten in the habit of telling her during their more heated discussions that, not being from this place, she knew nothing about it. That day, he would have felt wounded. "Go join the Communist Party then; with you there'll be enough to play bridge. Or go to the Maoists, there are half a dozen sects, take your pick. I'm tired of your European criteria." She would have shrugged. End that discussion. Talk about other things. Stop looking for trouble. They would quickly have made up by making love. In the midst of their caresses, he would say she was a goddamn Frenchwoman and would always be, and she would retort, hugging him, that he was a bumpkin and would always be. But she would feel that in the long run this type of confrontation would end up creating a rift between them. In the long run. How would she vote in the referendum? At times, she'd be almost sure she would vote yes. She would think of Maurice Audin and Henri Alleg and others who had fought for Algerian independence with the Algerians, who had carried suitcases for the FLN. Impossible to say NO, to vote with the supporters of the multinationals and the ruling class. At other times, however, on those frequent occasions when her husband would make her feel she wasn't from here, she would hesitate. Fear. Not the fear the Liberals were trying to instill—no, another fear.

> The fear of homogeneity
> > of unanimity
> > of the Us that excludes all others
> > of the pure

she the immigrant
> different
> deviant.

She would hesitate.
Because there could also be a Québécois way of witch hunting
because there could also be a Québécois way of being

xenophobic and anti-Semitic.
She would hesitate. Lost in this historic struggle
    not completely hers
    not completely other.

Strange convolutions, constraints, contradictions. Love it or leave it. Love it or maple leave it. Those anchor points in the murmured snatches of old memories. From now on, a time of elsewhere, of between-three-languages-and-three-alphabets in one day. Telescoped shifts from the great plains of Russia to the roofs of Paris, from the East End of London to the Lower East Side of New York, the Vistula, the Volga, the Volgule, virgule, comma, coma. Forgetting. Amnesia. Collages. Everything overlaps and mixes together. From now on, a time of confusion, contradiction, lonely despair. To make loneliness act. I loved the fall so much, the patches of red and chestnut through the luminous green, the piles of bright yellow leaves. This country spread its autumns before me. Brilliant. To wallow in, to gobble up gluttonously. The exhilarating rush of cold air, the smell of freshly cut grass, of acrid rotting leaves. Patches of blood red, scarlet, garnet, rust. The mountain on fire, wild as desire. The untamed mountain.

So I had imagined her in Outremont. But all that rang false. My pen balked. Inspiration ran out, the very sentences rebelled and refused to line up. None of it was credible. What, then? Was it impossible to integrate her, the Jacobin, the red, the communard? Impossible to *coquetieren* with this right-wing imagination, this right-wing heritage—the heirs of Louis Veuillot and Paul Bourget. Everything is called Lionel Groulx—new métro stations, university buildings, plaques on monuments. We—will—have—our—French—State—and—I—like—strong—States —and—corporations—and—leaders. Our race—*Action française —Action nationale*. Very little for me. Very little for her. Why not a monument to the Murdochville strikers, or to Fred Rose languishing in Warsaw! And the *fleur de lys* has strange connotations for her: royalist, anti-Semitic, a petty nobility imbued with its ancient privilege. I accuse du Paty de Clam and Darquier de Pellepoix and all the De's who were involved in getting us arrested in July 1942. She would know, however, that symbols have a history, that they can reverse their meanings, that they circulate in strange ways. She would never have been on the side of the dominators. She would be able to understand that here . . . she would want to understand. Would he give her the time?

But what am I meddling in, it's none of your business. Go get on your republican hobbyhorse. Go cultivate your French garden, the right to keep your mouth shut. Immigrants don't get involved in politics. The separations and wrenchings of History.

The right of peoples to control their own destiny.

Self-determination—of peoples, not only of bourgeoisies. MONTPARNASSE. Montparno. The long corridor to the métro before they installed the moving sidewalk. The Breton crêpe restaurants near the Tour de Montparnasse. The cafés—Le Dôme, Le Sélect, and the lemon pie at La Coupole. One day when you were fifteen, you waited for the great love of your adolescence at La Coupole, munching on lemon pie. He never came. You cried for an hour or two as one cries at fifteen, and walked aimlessly in the neighbourhood. Montparnasse! You took the métro. In the corridor a blind man was playing the accordion. You put in his box one of those 500-old-franc bills that don't exist any more. You sat on the platform for a long time looking at the advertisements. Montparnasse-Bienvenuë, spelled with a dieresis on the *e* or the *u,* I don't remember which. It was when they used to hold the Fête de l'Humanité in Vincennes, before the twentieth party congress. Being happy was still allowed.

Mime Yente would have absolutely insisted that she come to Snowdon every Friday for the Sabbath candles. Although an unbeliever, Mime Yente would have made up her own outrageously unorthodox personal ritual. While lighting the candles, she would recite the Sabbath blessing: "Joyful rest and light for the Jews, the Sabbath day is the day of delights. Those who observe and remember it can bear witness to this because in six days everything was called into being: the heaven of heavens, all the highest heavenly host and all the animals, the land and the seas, and finally man. Eternal God is a rock of protection and he speaks to his chosen people. Observe this day and make it holy from beginning to end: it is the very holy Sabbath. Joyful rest. . . ."

She would stand there listening to this prayer, a little irritated. She would have wanted to tell Mime Yente she couldn't stand rabbis any more than she could priests. Reading her thoughts, Mime Yente would have an answer for her: "Listen, it's a way of remembering you're Jewish. Never forget."

She would have to give in to her. Everything would be all right again during the elaborate Sabbath meal, with braided challah, gefilte fish, good hot soup, and tea. The samovar from Zhitomir would dominate one end of the table while at the other end Bilou would get the scraps. And so the evening would pass. She would like listening to Mime Yente tell old stories of the *shtetl:* Elijah crossing the market square on his white donkey or this story attributed to the Baal Shem or Peretz, she didn't remember which.

"A *tsaddik* was in the habit of going to a spot in the woods. He would make a fire, sing a certain song, and pray. People said that God generally did not remain deaf to his prayers.

"A generation later, the next *tsaddik* would go to the same spot in the woods, sing the same song, and pray, but he didn't know how to make the fire any more. It still worked.

"In the third generation, not only did the *tsaddik* not know how to make the fire but he couldn't remember the spot. He sang the same song and prayed to God, and it still worked.

"By the fourth generation, the place in the woods, the way of making the fire, and the song had been lost, but the story had not been forgotten, and the telling of it took the place of the action or, more precisely, the telling of the story *was* the action. For us, memory is an action."

She would stay for a long time, listening to Mime Yente and watching while she drank her tea, polished the samovar, filled her pipe, brought the strudel to the table, chided Bilou. "Play something on the piano," Mime Yente would say, picking up her knitting and sinking into a chair that looked like it too had survived from Zhitomir. Bilou would have pricked up his ears. In one leap, he would have been up on the sheet music to the right of the metronome. That evening she would have played a Mozart sonatina, one of the ones children are taught after only four or five years of piano. An old-fashioned melody, crystalline, gay, full of appoggiaturas. Mime Yente would keep time with her foot while knitting, her old pipe sitting in a garish ashtray from Miracle Mart.

"What are you teaching your students about now?" Mime Yente would ask, getting up to pour herself another cup of tea.

"About Kulbak," she would answer, her mouth full of strudel, "Kulbak's poem on Vilna."

> You are a dark amulet set in Lithuania.
> Figures smoulder faintly in the restless stone.
> Lucid, white sages of a distant radiance,
> Small, hard bones that were polished by toil.
> The red tunic of the steely *bundist.*
> The blue student who listens to grey Bergelson—
> Yiddish is the homely crown of the oak leaf
> Over the gates, sacred and profane, into the city.
> . . .
> And, on the old synagogue, a frozen water carrier,
> Small beard tilted, stands counting the stars.

A Friday night in Snowdon—the profound pleasure of being together.

Gedali, the Sabbath is passing

111

Gedali, who remembers?

That phantom character gets away from me. Impossible to fix in this urban geography, this moving space. As soon as she's moved in, integrated, she flees, moves away, forces me to break the story when I was just beginning to get into it myself, to enjoy it, to relax in it. She takes form and immediately flees, thumbing her nose at me. Do I know exactly where I'm taking her, lost among these conditionals, presents, and imperfects? Would I even be able, if I found her again, to finish the bits of her dreams, of her writing that she jots down from Paris to Volhynia? I hardly know her. Yet, like her at the beginning, you loved this country, you breathed more freely here than in Paris. This country seemed to you a place of female words, a place where women expressed themselves, perhaps even a place where they alone had anything to say, to shout. You had devoured that literature, had loved the boldness of its demands and its tone, its pleasure in writing. Writing was without a doubt the real country of these women in search of a country. Here, outside the heavy hierarchies of France, you'd be more relaxed in your woman's body—completely—equal—yourself. The women here had an air of freedom you had never known, a different relationship to their bodies. They didn't feel obligated to look like fashion plates. Young or old, beautiful or ugly, elegantly or casually dressed, in the métro, on the bus, on the main streets, at the entrances to stores or offices, they seemed to say to men: "That's the way it is. If you don't like it, tough luck." You liked their assurance, their ironic smiles, their newfound sureness. You who always walked close to the wall with your eyes lowered, you marvelled at the birth of this freedom. You the phony little French girl. "Look pretty and keep your mouth shut." But never having been pretty, you had been allowed, as an exception, to give your tongue free rein. Your body had been imprisoned, and here it seemed to you that your body was given back to you. Skin, nails, hair. For the

first time, you liked your body. New here. Relaxed—*shtiler,
shtiler*—so then why these stampedes from one place to another,
one language to another, one story to another, these jumps, these
flights, these returns, these regrets?

Basically, you've always lived in a language, and nowhere
else—those little black marks on paper that are read from right to
left. Those finely drawn letters. When you were little, you adored
the ש with its three little legs and the ל that reminded you of a
branch of lilacs. Your mother spent whole evenings reading those
books with the little brown marks running along in lines. You've
always lived in a language—in sounds that sometime ring Ger-
manic, sometimes Hebraic, even Slavic. A crossroads language,
wandering, mobile, like you, like her. To live in a language, an un-
translatable closeness. You've always lived in a poetic rhythm, a
way of breaking verses, breaking vessels, breaking anchor. A language in reverse, unlike others, going from right to left, with little
dots that the old editions from Vilna, from Drukarnia Wyd.
Wilenskie or B. Kleckina, respect to the letter. The little dot in
the פ that turns "f" into "p"; the וו with the little verticals; י the
"i"; וי the "oi"; ן the final "n"—funny signs. The signs of your
childhood, your mother, your only country this language. A language in reverse, going toward who knows what. A graphic image that is a whole landscape. A language of blood, death,
wounds, of pogroms and fear. A language of memory.

The Dinour River is said to be the river of Becoming. In this
indeterminate flight of signs, writing takes a detour.
Divulge. Writhing.
Reveal why in Hebrew the face is plural

פנם

PANIM, Words divided, broken.
> Multiple face
> multiple places, scattered.

The strategies of time and tense won't surprise you.
Gedali, time is passing. The Sabbath is passing

113

You will remain forever longing for the *shtetl.*

Something that refuses to be put in the imperfect or the past historic.

In the tenses of the dead. Of narrative.

Every story hides a corpse.

And the evening and the morning were—but morning was no more.

Death has only one face. It is German.

Der Tod.   דער טויט

Between the two words, all the difference.

From left to right. From right to left.

A *tess* is not a *t;* a ו is not an *o.*

Der Tod is a knight off to the Crusades—der Ritter—decimating everything in his path—the elves of the forest and all the gods of German mythology go with him. His eternally bloody sword is suspended forever over our heads.

דער טויט

is a voice that cannot be placed, that permits no metaphors. *Unrepresentable.*

There is no metaphor to signify Auschwitz, no genre, no writing. To write is to postulate a coherence, a continuity, a fullness of meaning somewhere. Even in the Beckettian absurd, even in the Kafkaian angst, the world still has shape, consistency, density. Nothing that can speak the horror and impossibility of living after. The link between language and History has been broken. The words are lacking. Language no longer has a source or a direction. What tense to use? There is only an eternal present. A present that does not pass. The weight of those millions of dead smothers me. Wandering from Europe to America with these burdensome dead demanding their due in a deafening silence. There is a mute impatience in their empty, earthy gaze. You're getting old, my friends. Yes, Manyale, you're already fifty-five years old—what have you done in all those years? Turned into

pollen, seed, dust carried by the wind, the birds, the bees? Yes,
Manyale, even in death, you don't get any younger. Don't worry.

> We'll all die for Carter
> and for the Afghan rebels
> for the rights of feudal man
> for his right to buy and sell his wife
> and all those peoples, who do they think they are?
> Those fanatical students in Teheran!
> We'll show them what oil we're made of!
> If ever we couldn't go to Florida any more
> in the winter or run our Chevrolets.
> World a thousand times free
>
> > CIA
> > FBI
> > RCMP

And question 32 to get into the United States.

> do you remember Sacco and Vanzetti
> > the Rosenbergs and
> > Fred Rose.
>
> A general consensus.
> Here we think Coke
> > 7-Up
> > ketchup and
> > Kraft dressing.
> Here we swim in sour cream
> > in Crescent yoghurt
> > in Sealtest milk.
> We'll all go and die for Exxon
> > and for Somoza
> > > for the Shah
> > > for Thieu
> > > for Stroessner
> > > for Pinochet
> > > for the murderers of Guevara

115

                                    and Letelier
                          for Begin and his colonies in
                          the occupied territories.
            Because the Kissingers of the world
            are all the same
            circling the world
            with PIDEs, SAVAKs, apartheid
            what do you want? We have no choice
                  it's that or the gulag, isn't it?
                  here we're right-thinking
                        we think   right
                  here we're public-spirited
                        we boycott Iranian restaurants
                              asshole Khomeini
                              nuke Iran.
            We throw vodka in the sewer
            we all dream of world war
                        Nuke Moscow, Dr. Strangelove.
            Finally a hot war
                        we'd missed it.
            Love it or maple leave it.
            It's sometimes hard simply to remain alive
            eyes open
                        waiting
            against—the—current
            in the outlawed BETWEEN-WORDS

    Her husband would have to spend most of the week in Que-
bec City. Her friends would often spend the evening by the hearth
in her beautiful house near Côte-Ste-Catherine. There would be
Latin Americans, Ukrainians, Greeks, Hungarians, and each
would bring something—Egri Bikavér, olives and feta cheese,
whiskey. They would spend entire evenings discussing the political situation here, telling jokes, talking about work, or simply

recalling people in their faraway countries. No stereotypes. The Latin Americans wouldn't have guitars, the Ukrainians wouldn't have banduras or balalaikas. No kitsch. They would have been here for a long time, in difficulty or in comfort. They would be her real country. Exiles, from nowhere, with no expectations, speaking every language and confronting every challenge of history. Their landscapes would at times weave a multicoloured patchwork. From the Pannonian plain to Patagonia, from the Black Sea to Piræus, they would have known all the skies and all the stars. She would play Bartók sonatas on the piano and everyone would identify—their flags and national anthems would weave together. They would be called "ethnics" to differentiate them from the Québécois and the English. Would she be comfortable as an "ethnic" on the nights when her husband was in Quebec City and she was transformed into an anglophone Jew laughing gaily with Ukrainians whose ancestors could have massacred her own family, with Hungarians who were descendants of old land owners, with militant revolutionaries who had been thrown out of Argentina? Her husband would sometimes find fault—but not in a nasty way—with the limited circle of her friendships. She would prefer the Quebec-Cuba Friendship Committee to the Société St-Jean-Baptiste, Fidel Castro to Duplessis, Guevara to Lionel Groulx, and Rosa Luxemburg to Marguerite Bourgeoys. To each, his or her own myths, symbols, and signs. Yet she would try by every means possible to grasp the political situation, to sense it. Day after day, he would repeat that, not being from here, she could never understand. She would finally have laid down her arms. Excluded. Alone in this collage city, this book city, this History city.

On the MAIN. SCHWARTZ HEBREW DELICATESSEN
    exciting smoked meats
    sizzling steaks and smiles
TURKEYS. Geese. SMOKED SPICED CHICKENS

assorted smoked meats
hot smoked meat.
                    ORDER early for the holidays.
Soft drinks—tomato juice.
On charcoal
                    prime rib steak with all the trimmings
                    liver steak
all sandwiches
black olives
pickles
our own French fries
smoked meat plate
Giant frank
                    Nash
Note all the differences, and the advertising with a taste of/for
Quebec
                    The caisse populaire
                    it's profitable . . .
                    for us Québécois.

            The strong point of a good vodka
            is its subtlety
                    Kamouraska has another strong point,
                    it's our own
            Kamouraska Vodka

            Let's cultivate our own garden
            and buy our own Quebec onions.
            Always fresh
            They guarantee great results.
            They're easy to recognize
            because their packaging
            says "Produce of Quebec" and shows the logo of the
            Quebec Onion Producers.
            Treat yourself to onions from Quebec.

Let us be the apple of your eye.
McIntosh and Cortland, with their bright red and
delicate green, are the most beautiful apples.
Beautiful and delicious.
Pick our Quebec apples—buy them by the bag.

The pleasure of walking in Outremont, going into Chez La-casse to see if they still had the pine and cedar chests or if they'd all been sold, going into all the stores on Laurier, losing herself in the streets with their luxurious homes on a day when the sky was pale blue and the air brisk. Taking Dunlop, passing the stone house with its greenhouse filled with red roses all year round, reaching the still chilly park, and then going back to Bernard, going into the Agence du Livre Français to look at the latest titles from Maspero, seeing what was playing that night at the Cinéma Outremont, making a dinner reservation for Saturday night at the Auvergnat or at Quinquet on St-Joseph, and walking slowly back to Côte-Ste-Catherine carrying a big bunch of irises.

Often on Saturday they would go to some bistrot on St-Denis with Québécois friends. Stripped wood was in style. Everybody on St-Denis would be busy renovating the gabled Victorian houses, stripping away the old varnish and paint to reveal the freshness of the natural pine. Pine and lace, salads with nuts and alfalfa, and flowers in old earthenware. She would call them the *stripniks,* borrowing the term with its Slavic ending from Mime Yente, who would have invented the concept of *stripnikeit* to describe the decor of the house near Côte-Ste-Catherine. St-Denis from south to north between Maisonneuve and Ontario on the east side.

VILLAJOIE CAFÉ
1887 Bar Restaurant
MAUVE Boutique
Charles E. Billard fils et métier à tissier
L'Alternatif

La chasse-galerie articles de cuir

TANGO

TWIST

LA GALOCHE Café

Le Saint-Malo Restaurant français

Le jardin Saint-Denis

BENOÎT BENOÎT: examen de la vue

Bar Picasso: restaurant

Le bistrot à JOJO

Épicerie Durette Licenciée

SALON DES CENT. BAR

LA BOÎTE À SON

LES JEANS SAINT-DENIS

RÔTISSERIE DU CAMPUS

NAPOLI PIZZERIA

MIKES SOUS-MARINS

LA COUR ST-DENIS

Librairie l'Ésotérique

PATRIMOINE SAINT-DENIS

BAR LES RETROUVAILLES

DISCO IN

AU VIEUX DU VIEUX

RESTAURANT VIETNAMIEN

DA CIRO RESTAURANT

LIBRAIRIE ROUGE

Pièces de moto toutes marques

STRIPTEASE L'AXE

TOPLESS DISCO SEX

LE PAVILLON DES ARTS

MATÉRIEL D'ARTISTES

LE CELTIQUE CRÊPES BRETONNES

La Revue du Grand Québec

LIBRAIRIE DÉOM

FORT-NET NETTOYEURS

The village. A Latin Quarter near the Université du Québec. Familiar names—Latin Quarter, St-Denis—and yet in the back of these cafés, she would feel much more out of place than on the Main. The words, the proper names, would be traps. She'd feel it. No sooner would they be seated in one of these places than she'd want to flee, to go to the Main or Snowdon with the Lithuanians, the Hungarians, the Portuguese, the Jews. There would be endless discussions of politics. She would try to understand but they wouldn't take her seriously. She would sulk. There would be no second Cuba in North America. She would be heartbroken.

PASTEUR. Near Rue Lacourbe and Rue des Volontaires. During an election campaign once, in a school gym. There were five of us against the Algerian War. We ended the evening a bit sad at the neighbourhood bistrot. At the counter the owner was singing the praises of Massu and the paratroopers. It was cold—

* * * * *

None of that is credible. Rhododendrons don't grow in Montreal. If her husband had really been a deputy minister, they would have lived in a nice house in Sillery. She would have had to entertain all year round and really get into the role of "wife of deputy minister." They would only have kept a pied-à-terre in Montreal. The house near Côte-Ste-Catherine was a little too luxurious. He should have had a different occupation and a more modest house in middle Outremont, with a facade facing east and a balcony full of lilacs opening onto a more traditional garden with roses and peonies, honeysuckle hedges, campanula and speedwell. What difference does it make? To portray an immigrant's imagination, you don't have to stick to reality. All right. He would be a psychiatrist or psychoanalyst, or both. The gabled house would have three floors, including a finished semi-basement. Large balconies with elaborate woodwork would get the morning sun. You'd enter by a double door of stripped wood with mauve and blue stained glass. The basement, consisting of a consulting room, a waiting room, and a bathroom, would actually be quite bright. On the ground floor there would be a large living room with inlaid woodwork, opening onto the dining room, the kitchen, and the garden. A pine staircase with a finely worked bannister would lead up to the second floor with its four bedrooms and bathroom.

She would have placed her piano prominently in the living room, opposite a blue velvet sofa. They would have bought an old wool rug, also in blue tones. An old pine chest would hold art nouveau lamps and trinkets brought back from trips to far-away places. The silver-plated menorah from Mime Yente would stand on the mantelpiece proudly holding up its seven silver-plated arms. There would be recliners and an easy chair, and German expressionist prints and lithographs on the walls— Marlene Dietrich in *The Blue Angel,* the blue horses of Franz Marc, and a violently coloured Nolde. In the dining room, an old Quebec table and six chairs, and a buffet completely restored but authentic, bought from the antique dealer on Greene Avenue, facing a china cabinet from Normandy. There would be ceramic pieces from the Revolutionary period brought back from France —the patriot, the revolutionary, Marat, and the friend of the constitution, each against a blue background. The effect would be simple, conveying unostentatious ease, the good taste of cultivated people who ignore social class and have no problems balancing their budget. She would have furnished the upstairs to her own taste, letting him make the decisions for the basement.

Her office would look out on the garden and receive the dying rays of the setting sun. It would be spacious and functional. An old refectory table in the centre would serve as a desk, and along all the walls there would be pine shelves and metal filing cabinets. She would have left only enough room, near the window, for two pictures, one of Kafka and one of Peretz Markish; she liked to gaze at the dark eyes of the former and the unruly mane of the latter. Books everywhere, file folders piled precariously, pencils and pens. In a corner, a low table with an IBM electric typewriter. In another corner, a walnut pedestal table with a big bunch of flowers that varied with the season, always in the same blue vase bought long ago in Prague. A brown carpet on the floor and a reclining chair. Lots of lamps and a clock. A bit of a shambles, but she would know where things were. At home. Their bedroom, next to her office, would be just like thousands of bedrooms of the Montreal upper intelligentsia. A big queen-size bed on one side, pine night tables, an old stripped armoire, an old dresser with white drawer pulls from Chez Lacasse, a modern beige wool carpet, a California patchwork quilt on the bed, and off-white lace curtains on the windows filtering the afternoon sunshine. The rooms on the east side would barely be furnished. The bathroom, with little tiles and an oval mirror hung horizontally, would have an old-fashioned look.

Along the front balcony there would be lilacs, rose bushes, junipers. The garden would be her secret pride. She would enjoy tending it daily, watching the crocuses, narcissus, daffodils, and tulips come up in the spring, impatiently awaiting the flowering of the hawthorn and the lilacs in June, delighting in the irises, poppies, roses, and peonies in the summer, enchanted by the many colours of the chrysanthemums in the fall. She would spend hours there in the warm weather, translating Soviet Jewish writers of the twenties and thirties. She would have been deeply moved by the words of a character in a story by David Bergelson. An old Jewish man comes back to his native village after the war. He meets a young girl who has also survived the slaughter. He speaks to her in Yiddish, and she translates his words into Russian. When she asks him if her translation is correct, he answers, "What can I say? The suffering was in Yiddish!"

He would have furnished the basement, which was actually quite bright and spacious, as an office for seeing his patients. The walls would be whitewashed to maximize the light. There would be naive paintings bought on the Rue de Seine in Paris and winter scenes by well-known Quebec painters—black-robed priests in an infinity of snow. A navy blue leather couch and chair and a walnut table covered with file folders and various objects. Next to the office, the waiting room, with bistrot chairs and a marble table holding a big bouquet of flowers that made you daydream. Another table with newspapers and magazines. An old clock with a brass pendulum like those in seventeenth century Dutch paintings, and on the wall, like a miniature echo, a Vermeer print. In that waiting room would sit people for whom the pain of living had become unbearable.

Every day they would have long discussions on international politics and Quebec, and she would be unable to make him understand her turmoil.

Watcher la game?

Put herself outside

between parentheses

between.

She'd feel that she would never really be able to live in this country, that she would never really be able to live in any country.

No place, no order.

Memory divided at the connections between words

The mute layers of language, broken

Immigrant words in suspense

between

two HISTORIES.

To go over to the other side,

passing through.

Those who have passed beyond.

The past unblinkered.

Gedali, nostalgia shouldn't be a return.

In the summer you liked to stretch out on the stone ledge facing the library with Kafka's letters to Milena as your pillow and let yourself drift off under the lacy canopy of translucent green maple leaves against the blue of the sky. An intense blue in the thick, almost viscous heat. Baseball players on the grass nearby, and the distant hum of traffic on Sherbrooke. From time to time the wind would shake the leaves of the maple, but otherwise all was blue stillness. You'd let yourself be filled with earthy thoughts from across the ocean, then you'd go back into the library. The materiality of the books—touching them, borrowing them, taking them out. Finding familiar passages. Feeling safe in the midst of books. An ancient store of knowledge, the print shops of Vilna. Death inhabits this language, a language with no future, with that turbulent past sticking to the delicate letters, a language with no present, frozen in its dismembered *shtetl*, a language swept away, with no destiny. Death inhabits this language metamorphosed into a sacred language, this language of the poor, of the people, of simple women. Knowledge stored on the shelves on the fifth floor of the library. The language is there with its alphabet, its syntax, its vocabulary, its dictionaries, its literature, its criticism. But no longer is there anyone to live in its everydayness, to wrap their secret thoughts or impossible points in it.

Gedali, who to write for?

Anywhere in the viselike city. Always, the strident music or the peace of winter, the smells of spices or of popcorn, the cheap relish or the macramé cafés. May as well stay in NDG, may as well not budge.

TO WANDER

You buy your ice cream at Tito Espresso Bar, your salads at Primo, and your ham at Henry's. You have your suits cleaned by the Polish Jew across from the bus stop. May as well not budge, forget your moments of weariness, regret, impatience, longing, your fleeting or lasting problems, your panics at the flight of the winter lines. May as well not budge.

TO WANDER

Note all the differences, make an inventory, a catalogue, a nomenclature. Register everything in order to give more body to this existence. Your slightest doings. Your encounters, your appointments, your movements. Forget nothing. Do not forget the menu of the Omelette Saint-Louis.

Omelette Émile Nelligan $2.95
(ham—cheese—tomato—onion)

Omelette La Bolduc $3.10
(ham—cheese—maple syrup)

Omelette Olivier Guimond $3.25
(bacon—ham—cheese—onion—nutmeg)

Omelette Amanda Alarie $2.75
(bacon—tomato—onion—herbs)

Omelette Marc-Aurèle Fortin $3.15
(chicken liver—bacon—tomato—herbs)

Omelette Ozias Leduc $2.95
(chicken liver—tomato—spinach)

Omelette Saint-Louis $3.95
*(ground beef—mushrooms—cheese—onion—
green pepper—herbs)*

Omelette Marie-Victorin $3.25
(chicken—mushrooms—tomato—herbs)

Omelette Théophile Hamel $2.75
(chicken—almonds—peppers)

Omelette Paul-Émile Borduas $2.95
(tuna—tomato—onion—herbs)

Omelette Arthur Villeneuve $3.75
(tuna—tomato—mushrooms—herbs)

Omelette Jean-Paul Lemieux $3.75
(shrimp—garlic—sour cream—parsley)

Omelette Antoine Plamondon $3.85
  (shrimp—asparagus—tomato—herbs)

Omelette Lionel Groulx $3.95
  (shrimp—avocado—sour cream)

Omelette Jos Montferrand $3.25
  (avocado—alfalfa sprouts—sour cream)

Omelette Saint-Denys Garneau $3.50
  (asparagus—ham—cheese)

Omelette Félix-Antoine Savard $2.85
  (zucchini—tomato—bacon)

Omelette Catherine Tekakwitha $4.15
  (scallops—mushrooms—cheese)

She would come to Snowdon every Friday night to see Mime Yente. She would sit at the piano for a long time. Bilou would get up on the sheet music at the right and purr, demanding Chopin. She would play old Ukrainian or Hungarian melodies to bring back the deeply buried past. Mime Yente, ensconced in her chair beside the samovar from Zhitomir with her pipe of shag tobacco in one hand and her cup of tea in the other, would close her eyes softly. She would sometimes resent her niece for bringing the dead shadows back to life, but she would let herself be lulled by the music, knowing that the niece adored Budapest and its light and would never give up its traditional melodies. Janos in days gone by on Margaret Island and the cafeteria near the Chain Bridge, and the smell of dead leaves, in days gone by. Bilou, equally overcome with emotion, would finally fall asleep curled in a ball on the sheet music up on the right. They would hardly speak, letting the sunflowers of Zhitomir and the cool, bright autumns of the Danube take shape between them. Both exiles, a little lost, with the samovar from Zhitomir. Zhitomir on the Teterev River.

Gedali, who remembers?

"What are you teaching your students about now?" Mime Yente would ask, picking up her knitting from the buffet. "A poem by Moshe Kulbak on Berlin in the twenties."

> "I am ailing, Mademoiselle.
> Like the century, I'm ailing.
> I who once made an amazing
> Leap from my father's threshold.
> Daring, young rage, impudence,
> Bits of Blok, Schopenhauer,
> Kabbalah, Peretz, Spinoza,
> Rootlessness and sorrow, sorrow.
> You wait away the years
> For your world to catch the lightning.
> Till your youth has driven by you.
> You sit there—left with nothing."

Summer or winter, they would take Mime Yente to their cottage a couple of hours' drive from Montreal, which they'd rent year-round. She would immediately have fallen in love with the purple expanse of the lake ruffled by the wind and the pungent birch woods surrounding it. She would immediately have known that she would get used to that pale light in the distance. In winter they would go snowshoeing on the lake. They would return in late afternoon, exhausted, intoxicated, stunned by the silence. They would like watching the sun bleed away into the icy expanse. Mime Yente would be waiting for them with a pot of soup steaming on the stove, one of her secret recipes from Zhitomir that she would never divulge. She would have put some logs on the fire in the living room fireplace. And so would begin the long winter evening, slow, cosy, sorrowful. The longing for Zhitomir would come over her from long ago. Not for London, where she and Moishe would have struggled so hard, not for Paris, where she would have gone to testify in the trial of Schwartzbard—no, for Zhitomir on the Teterev, for her father's house one *verst* from the town, a little whitewashed house lost in the midst of the sunflowers with the sun beating down on it, with an area in back where they built their hut of branches for Sukkot. Surrounded by gardens, and the town a *verst* away. Long ago, very long ago. Gazing at the frozen lake, she would wipe away a tear between two puffs on her pipe.

"I'll never see Zhitomir again, I'm too old now. There was a Jewish cemetery there near the tall acacia trees, with headstones of all shapes carved in beautiful limestone. Ach," she would say in a choked voice, "All that is dead. Maybe the house with the yellow shutters is still there, maybe."

She would have to be comforted. Bilou would crawl into her lap, and the niece, distressed, at a loss, far from her piano, would have to promise to take her to Zhitomir the next summer. Zhitomir in the Ukraine, Zhitomir in Volhynia, Zhitomir on the Teterev.

Sometimes, surrounded by colleagues or friends, she would be seized by a great panic. It could happen to her in a taxi, on a bus, in a restaurant, or while crossing the street. Is there nothing universal here?

GHETTOS
SPLITS
TO EACH HIS LANGUAGE
     HER COMMUNITY
TO EACH HIS NEIGHBOURHOOD
     HER ELECTED REPRESENTATIVE
HIS CAKE. HER NEWSPAPER. HIS RELIGION.
     HER FOLKLORE, HIS CUPS.
TO EACH HIS HISTORY
   ALONE
   APART
   WE.   YOU.   THEY.
Is there nothing universal here?
Skies split at the failure of History
     at the failure of exile

mauve solitudes confronting one other
                    facing one other
How far the sky is and what silence frosts the branches!
The text rustles with frozen imaginations.
Tell me, grandmother, why does the man on the television
        have such big teeth?
The better to eat you, my child.
What's good for Bombardier and Desmarais is good for
        Quebec.
Is there nothing universal here?

Yet in the thick of the crowd, no blue-white-red of the French flag, no crowing French cockerel, no military Marseillaise. You were waiting. For what? The handsome Che of your teenage years. The lack. Listening. Once upon a time there would again be countries of mimosa. Maybe!

Is there nothing universal here?

Taking advantage of a couple of strikes, she would have resumed work on her false messiahs.

Morton Himmelfarb, Morton sky-colour
would still be endlessly preparing his course. Forty-five hours on Sabbatai Sevi. Daydreaming in his study in the top-floor apartment near McGill University, the old asthmatic would be looking for ways around it.

Ish hayabi. Once upon a time. If they think it's so simple to tell a story, to tell History. There have been other crazies in Jewish history besides Sabbatai Sevi, other pathetic characters or mad geniuses who thought they were the Messiah, other shit disturbers inciting the poor and the widows and orphans to rebel. My death of a cold! With my health! My asthma attacks! To stay at the pine desk under the window. A good hot coffee. On Sunday morning, a nice cup of coffee and thick slices of bread with cream cheese and smoked salmon or whitefish. Outside, the snow. All these crazies of History! I'm feeling all right. Morton colour of a sad, wan sky is sensitive. He's getting upset. This damn course will cost him his life. Why not go back in history and show them that Sabbatai wasn't the first? Talk about those two rogues David Reubeni and Solomon Molcho, one of whom was burned to death at the stake by order of Charles V. Ah, Charles Quint! Of course, they don't know anything—what century, what dynasty, what country. Charles Quinsy. Charles Quintessence. Charles Quack Quack. They don't know anything. Got to tell them everything, the young Prince of Ghent, the imperial election, the Fuggers' cash, and so on and so forth. The Hapsburgs. The Holy Roman Empire. The Diet. One class. Joanna the Mad, that's picturesque, one class. Suleiman II at the gates of Vienna, one class. Charles V and the Protestants and Luther throwing his inkpot at the wall in the Wartburg. Good, maybe that will interest them, I don't know. The snow, to stay nice and warm in my study, in my bathrobe, with piles of books everywhere, with a nice hot coffee, and the empire on which the sun never sets in front of me with Carlos Quinto—not the paella king or the pizza king, no, the emperor. Don't know anything. Got to tell them everything, Yuste and the war against Francis I and the sack of Rome. And Titian's portrait. And what about the Jews in all this? Patience. Our two saviours are plotting in the shadows. Natasha, help me get my ideas organized. Fucked up, messed up, old Morton. Can't write History any more. Once upon a time there was a young Portuguese man born of Marrano parents, with a brilliant future, who began to study the Kabbalah in secret. Don't forget to say this was at the beginning of the sixteenth century. Very important, these chronological points of reference! Draw a picture of Mediterranean Europe in the sixteenth century. A map on the board, a little pedagogical arsenal, one class. Fourteen classes to go. A snowstorm, an asthma attack, or a strike —thirteen classes to fill. Natasha, help me. It's long. It's snowing. He met another young man, a bit of a dummy, who claimed to be a descendent of King Solomon through the tribe of Reuben.

Stop. Don't know anything, got to tell them everything. Solomon, that's okay. Some tribes, I'll say, ten in all, got lost in the desert on the other side of the Sambatyon River, which is impossible to cross. These tribes were supposed to be found again at the coming of the Messiah. Then there would be three days of darkness over Constantinople, but light in the dwelling places of the children of Israel. Recount the legend in a solemn voice. The Messiah would come back from the land of the exiled tribes on the other side of the Sambatyon. He would be mounted on a heavenly lion with a seven-headed serpent for a bridle, and he would be breathing fire. At that signal, all kings and all nations would bow down before him. He would arrive in Jerusalem at the western wall, which was believed never to have been deserted by the divine presence. On that day, all Jews who had died in Palestine would come back to life; those who had died in the Diaspora would come back to life forty years later. Show them that reality and legend are intermingled, and that the Jews believed this. A beautiful story. One class. Twelve classes to go, on the false Messiahs of the sixteenth century. My death of a cold! With my health! Natasha, you're so far away, so far! They met. Diego Pines, the Portuguese, wanted to become a Jew. He changed his name to Molcho Melech, meaning "king," and wanted to have himself circumcised. The other one, Reubeni, talked him out of it. It seems he circumcised himself. Uproar in the class, better skip this episode. He set out travelling and began to believe he was entrusted with a divine mission. He studied the Talmud, preached, gathered disciples, fired up crowds. The other one, meanwhile, told of his fabulous voyages, how he had been captured and sold into slavery to Arabs and taken to Alexandria, and then bought back by some Jews. He too started messianic propagandizing. Claimed to be the emissary of the king of the lost tribes of Israel on the other side of the Sambatyon. One class on his travels, the fantastic stories. Eleven classes to go. Nice and warm. Sunday morning at my desk with a good hot coffee, slices of bread with Philadelphia cream cheese and smoked salmon or whitefish, nice and warm at the window looking out on the highest branches of the maple tree. Natasha, help me. A two-room apartment, I think. Mama is spreading goose fat on kimmel bread. I leave for *cheder*. It's dark. I have to light my way with a lantern with a flickering flame. I'm afraid. What if the angel of death with a thousand eyes came after me! He said that to hasten the day of redemption, a certain stone in the western wall had to be moved, and that he was the only one that could do it. Went to Damascus, returned to Alexandria, left for Venice, and arrived in Rome in 1524 on a white horse and was received by Pope Clement VII. Said he was the commander in chief of the army of his brother, the leader of the ten lost tribes on the other side of the Sambatyon. Proposed a treaty of alliance with the pope against the Muslims in exchange for giving Charles V and Francis I letters for the kingdom of Prester John. Wealthy Jewish leaders raised money for him and gave him a silk banner embroidered with the ten commandments. So they were able to con rulers and popes, to play on their contradictions and penetrate the slightest cracks in their defences, and play on the legend and the belief in the coming of the Messiah. Morton sky-colour is getting bogged down. Don't know anything. Got to tell them everything. That the mysterious kingdom of Prester John was Ethiopia, and that Clement VII wasn't just anybody, but a Medici, the nephew of Lorenzo the Magnificent. Nothing to do with Saint Lawrence Street, I'll say. A real pope, who excommunicated Henry VIII of England. A real power, the pope, not just anybody. A leader of war as well. A head of state. Written test. You have two hours. Charles V abdicates. He's had it. He leaves everything to his brother Ferdinand and his son. He's had enough. In ten pages, explain why; you're not allowed to use your notes. You'll have to remember the important dates, the History, the dates—and silence please. One class for the written test. And our two saviours? Patience. The Jews have been waiting a long time for the Messiah, they can wait a little longer.

While Reubeni was looking for the stone in the western wall that had to be moved to bring the day of redemption, while he was raising an army, waving his banner with the ten commandments, Molcho was preaching—and convincing himself—that he was the Messiah. He had predicted the sack of Rome. He saw it as a sign of the times. I'll need one full class for Molcho—the beautiful story, the beautiful history of Elijah! Molcho the Messiah dressed as a beggar and spent thirty days and thirty nights among the crippled and the sick, eating almost nothing, living on the bridge over the Tiber opposite the papal palace, or at the doors of churches. That ought to remind them of something. You know, at the Passover seder, the glass that's poured and not drunk, the glass for the prophet Elijah, with the door left ajar in case Elijah comes back, as he promised, dressed as a beggar, a poor man among the poor. Woe to those who fail to recognize him and give him alms. You know that beautiful song that's sung at the seder, "Eliahu Hanavi." They all start singing. They're happy and so is old Morton. It takes up a quarter of an hour, and at least it's something they know, they have a point of reference. Natasha, help me get all this organized. Old Morton can't any more. Legend, History—how to differentiate them with all these messiahs, all these stories. Which is the true one? The true what, the true Messiah? Twice upon a time. First there were two, Reubeni and Molcho. Then Molcho went to the stake twice. Accused of Judaism by the Inquisition, he was sentenced to be burned at the stake in 1531. When the people heard of his death, they couldn't believe it. He, the Messiah, infallible, who had predicted the earthquake in Portugal and the floods in Rome, dead? He turned up in northern Italy the following year. He had been saved through the personal intervention of the Pope, and someone else had been burned instead. Digress here on the practices of the Inquisition, on the important people who all had their good Jews. After all, didn't Charles V extend the privileges of the Jews of Alsace to all Jews in the Empire after the dispute between

Margarita and Gershom of Rosheim? I've lost track of how many classes now. Plan for another asthma attack. Don't leave our two heroes until after their deaths, follow them step by step through their processions on horseback, their mad schemes, their hope. In Portugal the king gave Reubeni a triumphal reception befitting an ambassador. The Marranos flocked to kiss his hands. Was he not the herald of the Messiah? During his travels he had awakened great hopes. He had tried to raise a Jewish fleet to attack Jerusalem. As for Molcho, he continued his apocalyptic propagandizing. Natasha, the ideas are all mixed up in my head. No order, no logic, no chronology, no lodging. I don't know any more. They're going to laugh at me. In 1532, yes, I was in 1532. Molcho, with his banner with Hebrew inscriptions in a gold triangle, went to Ratisbonne. He wanted to talk to the emperor. Maybe pause here and explain that until then our two buddies had a lot of protectors, including the pope and the king of Portugal. Why not the emperor? Molcho's plan was to get Charles V to call on the Jews to fight the Turks. They would raise an army and a fleet, and take Jerusalem, the bulwark of civilization against the Muslim peril. They had been talking about this idea for a long time. A false messiah, maybe, but a political false messiah. From there, History took a bad turn. Reubeni clashed with the Portuguese nobility and had to flee. He was imprisoned in Spain and escaped. He was imprisoned in Provence, and freed after the Jewish community of Avignon and Carpentras paid a ransom. Arrested again in Spain in 1532, he died in 1538, completely alone, without having succeeded in finding the right stone in the western wall. The emperor was in Ratisbonne presiding over the Diet. He had Molcho arrested all the more quickly because his reputation extended beyond borders, and the poor—and not only the Jews — considered him the Messiah. Having refused to convert to Christianity, Molcho was burned in Mantua in 1532. Once again it was believed that someone else had been substituted for him, that he was safe and sound, galloping to Jerusalem on his white horse with Reubeni, banners flying, to announce the news and move the stone in the western wall. The people waited.

They will wait, Natasha!

They're still waiting!

Once upon a time. Beautiful stories. To tell stories, or to tell History . . . . . .

The sky moves
Runs, cut loose,
The ancient lyric breath is dead.
The skeleton of dead words smothers
in the viscous summer.
city of shadows!
The heart pounds against the words that cannot be invented
always at the edge.
Vain detours,
vain departures,
vain returns.
And the evening and the morning were
without end,
Nothingness,
the heart pounds without end
in the thick of the crowd
dull
rust city

Ask her anything—
almost.

After Grenelle, I don't know any more
the line gets lost in my memory
the operation was called spring wind
around Rue du Dr Finlay
Rue Nocard
Rue Nelaton
in the 15th arrondissement.

It was nice out that *finstere donershtik*
that grim Thursday
that July 16, 1942.
Gedali, who remembers.
The skies there are so fragile.
The noises are gone
it's the same sky again.
Evenings to make you scream.
                    Weariness.
The light no longer calls.

How would their story have ended? I don't know. One day
she would have decided to leave. It wouldn't even have occurred
to Mime Yente to stop her. She would have taken an Air France
747 leaving from Mirabel at 20:45. Her books and personal ef-
fects would follow by air freight, and some pieces of furniture by
boat in a container.
She would have taken the métro again. To Grenelle.
       France would have changed.
No order. No chronology, no logic, no lodging.
       The connections are screwed up.
       There will be no messiah.
       There will be no story.
       Nothing will have taken place,
       no place,
just barely a plural voice
               a crossroads voice
               a voice of the other where an underwater rock breaks
               the flow of the text
               immigrant words.

III

Around the Marché Jean-Talon

On the Alexanderplatz they are tearing up the road-bed for the subway. People walk on planks. The street-cars pass over the square up Alexanderstrasse through Münzstrasse to the Rosenthaler Tor. To the right and left are streets. House follows house along the streets. They are full of men and women from cellar to garret. On the ground floor are shops.

Liquor shops, restaurants, fruit and vegetable stores, groceries and delicatessen, moving business, painting and decorating, manufacture of ladies' wear, flour and mill materials, automobile garage, extinguisher company: The superiority of the small motor syringe lies in its simple construction, easy service, small weight, small size.—German fellow-citizens, never has a people been deceived more ignominiously, never has a nation been betrayed more ignominiously and more unjustly than the German people. Do you remember how Scheidemann promised us peace, liberty, and bread from the window of the Reichstag on November 9, 1918? And how has that promise been kept?—Drainage equipment, window-cleaning company, sleep is medicine, Steiner's Paradise Bed.—Book-shop, the library of the modern man, our collected works of leading poets and thinkers compose the library of the modern man. They are the great representatives of the intellectual life of Europe.—The Tenants' Protection Law is a scrap of paper. Rents increase steadily. The professional middle-class is being put on the street and strangled, the sheriff has a rich harvest. We demand public credits up to 15,000 marks for the small trades-man, immediate prohibition of all public auctions in the case of small tradesmen.—To face her hour of travail well prepared is the desire and duty of every woman. Every thought and feeling of the expectant mother re-volves around the unborn. Therefore the selection of the right drink for the mother-to-be is of especial impor-tance. Genuine Engelhardt Stout and Ale possess, above all other drinks, the qualities of palatability, nutritious-ness, digestibility, tonic vigour.—Provide for your child and your family by contracting a life insurance with a Swiss life insurance company, Life Annuities Office, Zürich.—Your heart is light! Your heart is light with joy, if you possess a home equipped with the famous Höffner furniture. Everything you have dreamed of with regard to pleasant comfort is surpassed by an un-dreamed-of reality. Although the years may pass, it will always look well and its durability and practical wear will make you enjoy it continuously.—

The Private Protective Agencies watch everything, they walk around buildings and through buildings, they look into buildings, control clocks, Automatic Alarms, Watch and Safeguard Service for Greater Berlin and environs, Germania Protective Agency, Greater Berlin Protective Agency, and former Watch and Ward Divi-sion of the Café Proprietors' Association of the Society of Berlin House-Owners and Landlords, Associated Management, West Side Central Watchmen's Service, Watch and Protection Company, Sherlock Company, collected works of Sherlock Holmes by Conan Doyle, Watch and Protection Company for Berlin and adjacent towns, catch it in time, Watch on the Rhine . . . .

—Alfred Döblin, *Alexanderplatz Berlin*

I HAD TRIED. Again. But I knew it. It was bound to end badly. Might as well give her to the ethnics, the halfbreeds she's so at home with. Not in Outremont, not in Westmount. Swann's way as closed as that of the Guermantes. all right, then! But I did try. Impossible to fathom this city, to assimilate it, to make it part of you. Impossible simply to stop somewhere, put down your packsack, and say phew! Like her, you too loved losing yourself in the city, blending into its everyday bustle, living to its sounds. It's daylight. The sun is still weak but it will be a warm day. Far off in the sky, a trail left by a plane. Cars are starting in the street. A baby cries. Further away, some voices in argument. The sound of an electric coffee grinder. Soon the smell of bread toasting. The sun comes into the bedroom. The city is heavy, heavy. Get dressed, have breakfast, leave and lose yourself anywhere in any neighbourhood. Walk, wander, or maybe not budge. The city is stirring. The sun warms the balcony. The toast is ready. You have lost your age and your name. You're only this ray of sunshine, these scarcely opened buds that are filling the balcony. You are only the low murmur of this city without coherence, without unity. To try once again to grasp this impossible city, to confront the icy winters and hot, humid summers, once again to wander.

Would it be necessary to start all over again?
Give her a new neighbourhood, new prospects?
Find her a new lover, another occupation?
Try one more time, but the heart wearies.
It's fed up.

This will be the last.
Gedali, protect her.
One more time, alone, across this city
across this island
in the middle of the American ocean.
Gedali, protect her.
Help her not to despair
not to waste herself
to keep on believing.
Gedali, who to write for?

She would have met him at a Quebec-Cuba Association evening in honour of the Sandinistas' struggle in Nicaragua. The band would have been playing sambas, rumbas, and tangos from another time. There would have been a big crowd. At the door, a table with books for sale, in English or Spanish, on Cuba, Nicaragua, and Latin America in general, studies by progressive Americans on the Trilateral Commission, the CIA, and American activities in Latin America. Books of poetry by Latin Americans, as well. She would have spent a long time at the door leafing through them. He would have been running the refreshment stand at the back near the band, as brown as the musicians, with an absent look although he was busy. He wouldn't have had a moment free, serving Cokes and 7-Ups, juices, sandwiches, tacos, and tortillas. After dancing a few tangos, she would have gone to the counter and ordered a Coke. She would instinctively have spoken to him in Spanish. He would have smiled at her mangling of the language with her French accent. Serving her Coke, he would slyly have asked where she had got that delightful accent, where she was from. It was perfectly simple: she was a Ukrainian Jew from Paris living in Montreal temporarily, teaching in the anglophone universities, who had learned Spanish at the lycée in Paris. Phew! They would both have laughed.

"Yes, I can see how simple it is," he would have said.

"But what about you, that must be clearer?"

"Sure. I'm Paraguayan, from Asunción. I fled Stroessner's prisons. And I washed up here, so to speak. I'm a worker in a cardboard factory, non-unionized of course."

They would again have laughed at the same time. Then there would have been a silence in the room. The refreshment stand would be deserted, people would be gathered to listen to a representative of the Sandinistas. He would thank the Montrealers for the money they had been collecting for months and bring greetings from the fighters, promising that Somoza would soon be crushed. Waves of enthusiasm in the room.

"One day Stroessner will get his, and then I'll go back to Asunción," he would have said with conviction, his expression serious, his gaze far away. Then the music again. He would have got someone to replace him at the stand and asked her to dance some tangos. She would have felt at home in the midst of this old-fashioned music, in the midst of the smoke. They would have said goodbye to the organizers and the Sandinista representative, who seemed to be an old acquaintance of his. He would have invited her for dinner at an Italian restaurant in his neighbourhood.

"I live on St-Laurent near Jean-Talon, near the Marché Jean-Talon. Do you know the area?"

She would have nodded yes, although she had never set foot in it. She would have been delighted to discover it with him.

The pizzeria would be simply but attractively decorated, very bright, with colourful tablecloths on the tables. She would have been unable to hide her surprise at hearing him speak Italian to the owner or manager.

"Oh, yes, I know Italian. A lot of the workers I work with are Italian. We're trying to form a union. It's tough. The pizza is excellent here. Real Neapolitan pizza. Not that thick crust you usually get. You should try it."

"What's Asunción like?" she would have asked him, biting into a delicious seafood pizza while he poured Valpolicella.

He would have looked at her with his dark eyes hard and impenetrable. She would have found him attractive, knowing he must be feeling the same about her. She would have pretended not to notice, savouring the anticipation of what was to come, delighting in these delicate moments before the declarations, when everything still seemed uncertain but you already knew that a relationship was beginning.

"Asunción. That depends. It's not very big. A nice city, founded by the conquistadors where the Pilcomayo meets the Paraguay."

"Names that make you dream," she would have said, a little tipsy. "I've always loved the names of rivers. For example, my Aunt Yente comes from Zhitomir on the Teterev. That's nice too, isn't it?"

"A tropical city. You've no idea of the heat in Asunción in the summer, when it's winter here."

"Tell me more."

"What can I tell you? In 1954, Stroessner came into power. There's been fascism there since then. I did five years in prison. The houses in Asunción are white. I was in the underground. Later I went to Argentina and then to Chile to get away from Stroessner. I was in Santiago when Allende was elected. I think that and Fidel's victory in Cuba were the most beautiful days of my life. And then, Pinochet and all that. I came here with the Chilean refugees, but I had a hard time. You have to have papers to get in. Yes, the houses in Asunción are low and white. But why talk about that?—we're having a good time. I like this place. The owner gives me credit. He subscribes to *Unità*."

"You mean there are communists among the Italians in Montreal?" She would have blushed at her question. He would have smiled and continued pouring Valpolicella. She would have been flustered.

"I meant . . ." She would have burst out laughing again.

The evening would have gone on gently in a delightful state of intoxication. He would have questioned her in his turn, and after her first few answers, asked her to recite poems in Yiddish, Hungarian, Russian, or Ukrainian. She would have done so with pleasure, speaking rather loudly and arousing the curiosity of the people at the neighbouring tables, all good-humoured Italians.

"Exactly why did you come to Montreal?" he would have asked her, signalling the waiter to bring the menu and taking a pipe and tobacco out of his pocket.

"Does one ever know why one finds oneself elsewhere?" she would have replied, suddenly weary, almost sad.

"I know why," he would have answered, his eyes hard.

"Yes, for you it's clear, but for me it's complicated. Maybe it doesn't matter. Here or elsewhere, I've never felt at home. You know what I mean. I don't really have a home, and besides . . ." She would have stopped to look at the menu and order some gorgonzola. He would have agreed and ordered another bottle of wine. "And besides, I like wandering. I like always being else-where. You know what I mean, don't you?"

It would be getting late. In a few hours, they would have dis-covered everything about each other. They would feel a magnet-ism between them. Between the gorgonzola and the zuppa inglese, they would have decided never to part.

Charenton—Place Balard.

Line number 8. BASTILLE. La Bastoche. The storming of the Bastille and Nini Peau de Chien. It was still a working-class neighbourhood then. You liked to walk back along Rue du Fau-bourg Saint-Antoine to La Nation through the woodworkers' quarter, the old neighbourhood of the *sans-culottes*. Its blind streets and courtyards reminded you of Eugène Sue and the treacherous area between Rue de Lappe and the Impasses de la Main d'Or in the nineteenth century. That was the way you would take to go visit your uncle up near Hôpital Saint-Antoine.

His house was between the dairy shop run by a chubby woman who had the best Brie, and a sad florist who had killed himself, leaving a final ironic note: "No flowers or wreaths." The uncle would give you ten sous and you'd go down and buy roudoudous and barley sugar candy.

Every year on July 14, the Place de la Bastille was transformed. There were tricolour flags and paper lanterns everywhere, and refreshment stands and accordion bands. The people all wore liberty caps and danced the *java vache*. The uncle taught you the java and bought you huge balls of cotton candy and lemonade. And then there were the speakers. All reds. They spoke of '89 and '93, and the Paris Commune. All you remember is the end of their speeches, which never changed from year to year: "There are a lot of Bastilles still to be stormed!" and then the *Internationale*. "They soon shall hear the bullets flying, we'll shoot the generals on our own side." You sang your lungs out on that verse, your mouth full of cotton candy and your left fist raised, loving it. You were twelve years old at the time of the big demonstration against Ridgway. The Bastille, the blaring music, and the cotton candy.

> Low skies before the snow,
> grey, invisible.
> > Waiting.
> Throughout a city, silence.
> Wooden porches and balconies. Iron fire escapes.
> Brick painted bright red, apple green
> Crooked roofs, shapeless.
> Colourful chaotic maze.
> The Saint Lawrence frozen like a cracked green and grey moiré
> Low skies. It is dark
> It is silent.
> Everything is crouched in waiting.

The city is on its guard.
It's going to snow.
The children hurry home
the squirrels have hidden
the cars speed up.
Heavy snow warning.
That time, storm.
Winter in Montreal.

She would have insisted on moving in with him in spite of
the grumbling of Mime Yente, who would have wanted to keep
her in Snowdon, and in spite of Bilou's disdainful faces. His
apartment would be on St-Laurent at Jean-Talon, up an outside
staircase that was quite dark. It would consist of three large ir-
regularly shaped rooms that were dark and damp, plus a kitchen
and bathroom. He would have had it painted when he moved in
but the colours would have faded. The rather large rooms would
be furnished sparsely and humbly. The front room would be a
cheerless living room, with an old wicker couch and a creaky
rocking chair facing a television set. But there would be a shiny
new hi-fi system and lots of records of Latin American music. A
rug whose colours had faded would hide the pattern of a lino-
leum from another era. There would be a buffet of imitation teak
with a bronze bust of Lenin on it that was also a survivor of
Stroessner's prisons. From the window you'd see the Main, a bit
sad and sickly at this level.

    Roma Groceries
    Chez Ubaldo
Parc Martel   Casa Napoli
             Casa del formaggio
Rimini
Engels   Milano
             Mobili Torino
    Cycles Baggio

Chez Dino: Hamburger, patates frites
Restaurant Frascati

An Italian Disneyland. A real or a phony Italy, how could you tell? The need to be together, to evoke the country, the town, the village? Perhaps!

The entry hall would lead to two other rooms. His bedroom would face east and get the morning sun, with a beautiful Mexican blanket on the bed and a night table from the unpainted furniture place on Rue Beaubien, which he wouldn't have gotten around to finishing, a lopsided wardrobe that was quite big, and a mirror that added a touch of cheer. The other room, which would become her office as soon as she moved in, would be half empty, serving as storage space. The bathroom would offer the basic amenities in spite of the lack of water pressure. As for the kitchen, there was nothing to complain about. It would have every convenience of the American way of life: a large fridge taking up fully a quarter of the room, a stove, shelves, cupboards, and a large sink.

The rent would be very low. Over the years he would have become attached to his "hole," taking a liking to the neighbourhood and enjoying wandering the streets around the market on summer Sunday mornings.

"The damp reminds me of Asunción," he would have joked when she arrived with her many boxes of books, her files, her IBM electric typewriter, bricks and boards for instant bookshelves, and a door from a construction site to set on trestles to make a desk. It wouldn't have taken her long to get settled, to furnish the second bedroom and put up a poster of *The Blue Angel*, a picture of Kafka, and a huge reproduction of an eighteenth century map of Paris. She would have made him let her liven up that dreary apartment a bit. With her savings and some help from good Mime Yente, she would have bought new curtains, some of gauze and some of lace, a few secondhand rugs, a nice old chest of drawers found at a flea market, a Québécois armoire she would have paid for on credit, and finally a piano, also second-hand but properly tuned, which they would have put in the living room with a big vase of flowers on it. She would have insisted on having flowers everywhere. He would have let her have her way, amused, uneasy, won over.

"You're my sun, my garden," he would have murmured in Spanish, hugging her, "You've made this hole a real home, an oasis. Come listen to some Paraguayan music." She'd sit down on the old wicker sofa, determined to replace it with something else at the first opportunity, even if it was only foam that she'd cover with a nice fabric. She would let herself be seduced by this strange, faraway music, piercing and rhythmic. In his rocking chair, with his pipe of shag tobacco in his mouth, he would close his eyes. He would be grateful for her silence. Where would he be at those times? What would he be remembering from Asunción? His former life, his childhood? Stroessner's prisons, his escape? That was something he would rarely talk about.

Note all the differences. Leave nothing to chance.

Above all, do not ignore anything.

Remember the names of the strange political parties from elsewhere.

Liberal Party
Progressive Conservative Party!!!!!!!!!
Union Nationale
Social Credit
New Democratic Party
Parti Québécois

At first, when you saw PC in a newspaper headline, you would have stared at it amazed. The Communist Party here? It took you a while to realize that here these initials stood for Progressive Conservatives, not Parti Communiste. Oh, okay!

Yes, note all the differences. Forget nothing, not the brands of toothpaste, the chains of barbecue restaurants and pizzerias, the brand names of soap and detergent. Penetrate the strangeness of this everyday life. In exile in your own language. The trickery of the language. Neither the same nor other.

The OTHER in the SAME
The disquieting strangeness of here.

On weekdays he would get up at dawn to take the bus to work in the cardboard plant at the other end of the city. He'd come back around seven. When he was on the day shift. When he was on the night shift, they would hardly see each other. He would rarely talk about his work on the assembly line. She would infer his pain from his fatigue, and from the sight of his hands, which were swollen and sometimes had running sores on them that were hard to treat. He wouldn't complain; he knew that in this country he would always be a second-class citizen. Immigrants don't get involved in politics. He would have been refused Canadian citizenship because he was marked as a subversive, a threat to national security. He would have known. Prudently, he would spend his remaining energy in efforts to unionize and social activism in the Latin American community. In connection with the latter, he would take one or two trips to Mexico to make contact with Argentinians or Chileans newly arrived there. She would have promised herself that she'd go with him on the next trip.

She would have found a few courses to teach for starvation wages in one of the city's anglophone universities. She would talk to the fascinated students about Soviet Jewish poetry of the twenties. She would have spent a lot of time discussing this extract from a long poem by Kulbak:

My grandfather in Kobilnik is a plain man,
A peasant, with a furskin coat, an axe and a horse,
And my sixteen uncles, and their brother, my father,
Are plain folk, like clods of earth, lumpish and coarse.

They float rafts on the river, haul timber from the forests,
Toil hard like beasts of burden all day,

They eat supper together, all out of one basin.
Then fall into bed, and sleep like lumps of clay.

My grandfather can hardly manage to crawl
To his corner on the stove; he falls asleep there.
His legs carry him on their own to the stove.
They know the way, this many a year.

On summer Sundays they'd like nothing better than to spend hours wandering around the Marché Jean-Talon. Sometimes for a moment she'd think they were in Naples or Sicily. He, with a little imagination, would sometimes be reminded of the markets in small towns in Paraguay. There would be mounds of tomatoes, cauliflowers, lettuces, and peppers, straw baskets full of blueberries or strawberries, and further on, braids of garlic, red and white onions, shallots, herbs. There would be the scent of fennel, thyme, and mint amidst the flies and wasps, between the slightly sour watermelons and the prickly pears from who knows where. Still further, flowers and plants, mellow odours wafting over the voices speaking Italian and Greek. A cheerful confusion they'd feel at home in, delighting in the array of honey and natural jams, jars of wild garlic, sachets of lavender.

They would carry their purchases upstairs and then go out again to Milano for fresh pasta, feta cheese, and olives. For lunch, they would go back to the pizzeria where they had first gotten to know each other, and then they'd walk in the neighbourhood around Parc Jarry or down the Main to Beaubien, Rosemont, or even Laurier, meeting Italian, Latin American or Québécois friends. They'd come back home and make love on the carpet in the living room. She would love the way he murmured in her ear in Spanish. Then for hours, in the calm of the late afternoon, she would play the piano, that old secondhand piano with its crystalline tone. He'd be sitting in his rocking chair listening, pipe in hand, surrounded by piles of Latin-American underground publications.

MÉTRO RÉPUBLIQUE, an important station. Everyone transferred there. You had to go through a long corridor for the train to Mairie des Lilas. On Sunday, regardless of the weather, we got together in the square. At fifteen, the routes you take are not original. We all took the *grands boulevards* to the Boulevard des Italiens. The Place de la République in front of the Toile d'Avion department store or the modern hotel. Later, you once spent hours there waiting for Janos. You'd made a date to meet there. He'd been wanting a nice choucroute for a long time. You had reserved a table at Chez Jenny. You arrived early and ordered a pastis to kill time, nervously smoking one Gauloise after another. You had met Janos at the conservatory in Budapest in the fall. He was a music teacher and nobody could play Kodály or Bartók like him, on the piano, violin, or cello. He had gone through the events of 1956 without too many problems, understanding nothing, living only for his music, for that city he loved so much, and for his house on Rózsadomb, Rose Hill—which was incredibly charming, opening onto a garden with lilac hedges and climbing rose bushes—living only to tramp through the dead leaves on Margaret Island and watch the boats go by on the Danube. Janos was late. You didn't know what to think. From the table where you waited sadly, you looked out at the Place de la République. It was raining. Umbrellas, overcoats, puddles, and the brakelights of the cars at the traffic lights. You looked out at this Paris of the end of your adolescence. Already wandering. In Paris or in Budapest? What for? Janos did not come that night, or any other night. He had gone back to Budapest early. He would write much later to tell you. He had fled, knowing that if he came to see you that night, he would give it all up for you, his country, his house, the conservatory and his music. You stayed alone at Chez Jenny on the Place de la République for hours. After paying the bill and leaving, having for appearances ordered a choucroute you didn't touch, you took the métro—République, toward Porte des Lilas. Never again the lilacs on Rose Hill in Budapest, never again Janos's childlike gaze. Cities seek and answer each other in the night. Sometimes they resemble each other. Paris or Budapest.

Budapest or Paris. Or Montreal. What does it matter! Somewhere in the imagination of the city!

The text is getting away from me. I feel it slipping away. Secretions of the picturesque, bleeding. Cheap nostalgia. Illusions of rootedness. This character is eluding me again. I get caught up in her story. I end up believing in the reality of Mime Yente and her cat Bilou, I end up wanting to follow a plot, a semblance of a story with a beginning and an ending. I find myself wanting a bit of order, of logic, a place, something. Living in little steps, last gasps. Time—to drag myself around day after day. Errands to do—as they say here, shopping. Stringing together movements, scraps of city, of void, of life. I end up longing for story. Where to take her? After all, she can't live in every neighbourhood in Montreal. Keep walking her around like this in the city of melancholy evenings, deepening shadows? From the Marché Jean-Talon to Verdun, from Pointe-aux-Trembles to Old Montreal? Waiting, broken? Give her lovers of every nationality—and then? There will still be exile, the eternal feeling of being elsewhere, uprooted. Montreal or Paris, Budapest or Zhitomir or New York. Cities seek and answer each other in the night. Sometimes they resemble each other. What does it matter! Somewhere in the imagination of the city.

I feel completely trapped by her. She ends up taking me by the hand and guiding me. If I give her some face or some fate, she rebels. She's the one that ends up giving the orders. She wants her place, her whole place. She won't accept being a shadow, a mere prop for writing. No. She leaves the paper, taking her *barbudo* and Mime Yente and Bilou with her. She thumbs her nose at me. She moves in. Yes, moves in. To stay somewhere. The temptation of pure breeding, a nice passport, genealogy, the "I, my ancestors here two hundred, three hundred years ago, my nobility going back to the time of the Crusades, this land worked by my forebears, etc." That's for others! We've heard it before. I have no forebears. All dead at Auschwitz, and before that, little, obscure, ordinary, anonymous. No forebears, just elsewheres. Yes, she eludes me. Probably tired of this mad rush across the city, of this novel that she can't finish.

false messiahs and
false stories

Yes, tired. Budapest or Paris, Paris or Budapest or Montreal. What does it matter! It has no end.

Friday nights would belong to Mime Yente. They would go to Snowdon, bringing her flowers. She would light the candles of the menorah and they would celebrate the Sabbath. Mime Yente would pour a glass of wine and declaim in Hebrew, clutching her pipe of shag tobacco. "And the evening and the morning were the sixth day. Thus the heavens and the earth were finished, and all the host of them. And on the seventh day God ended his work which he had made; and he rested on the seventh day from all his work which he had made. And God blessed the seventh day, and sanctified it: because that in it he had rested from all his work which God created and made." They would have an elaborate dinner by the light of the candles of the menorah. The aunt would put the small plates on the larger ones. They would feast on gefilte fish, knaidlach, blintzes with sour cream, and strudel, all washed down with tea. Because the samovar from Zhitomir would always be there. And Bilou would be under the table picking up the crumbs and curling up at the feet of each of them in turn. Mime Yente would immediately have adopted that black-eyed *barbudo* from out of Stroessner's prisons. He would have told her of the struggles he'd been in, the victories and the defeats, and she would have told him all about the Ukraine, Petlyura's pogroms, her escape to London, and the Schwartzbard trial in Paris. They would have understood each other perfectly. Veterans, old soldiers sidelined. They would have had a lot of other things in common, like their pipes and shag tobacco. On Friday nights, she would play old songs for Mime Yente and Chopin for Bilou curled in a ball up on top of the sheet music at the right. They would talk about the political situation in the world, in Latin America, in Canada, and in Quebec. They would never tire of talking about the past.

"You should move," Mime Yente would say regularly. "It's too damp there. You should find a place around here." They wouldn't say anything because they were attached to the Marché Jean-Talon and the local pizzerias and Italian grocery stores, which to them were irreplaceable.

"We'll see," she would answer between sips of tea. "We'll see later." They would leave Mime Yente quite late in the evening for the long haul home by bus and métro. On summer nights, they would walk to the corner of Sherbrooke and St-Laurent and only take the bus up the Main. Or else they would go all the way home on foot, taking a winding route. They would love walking in the city, listening to its languages, its transformations, its noises. From Snowdon they would take Lacombe to Victoria, following it way up north, dreaming of houses of stone or brick, looking at the brightly lighted interiors with beautiful fringed lampshades and plants in the windows. They would continue along Victoria to Van Horne and sometimes further, to the heart of the Jewish neighbourhood:

Spaghettiville	Bagelville
Royal Bank	Brown Derby
Pharmaprix	Victoria Trust

Everywhere, kosher butcher shops, synagogues, houses of prayer, congregations. Bagelerie Van Horne, Budapest Grocery, Marché Aviv. Then they would go through Outremont, passing the beautiful houses on Pratt Park. It would be silent. Further on, the sleeping neighbourhood would change into a more working-class area. They would go north up St-Laurent until they reached home. It would be a very long walk that seemed to take them to the ends of the earth. They would only undertake it on certain summer nights, nights when there was a light breeze that smelled of lilacs, in June, or of roses, later, wafting from the gardens around the houses. They would only feel completely themselves when walking, crossing the different neighbourhoods.

"You leave one ghetto and enter another," he would mutter ironically, "the Jews, then the rich, then the Italians. Nothing but ghettos. Did you notice?"

She would have noticed. Forever in a ghetto, never having managed—in spite of everything—to get out, remembering some lines by Glatshteyn, the American Jewish poet, and reciting them for him in the warm night.

> Good night, wide world,
> great, stinking world.
> Not you, but I slam the gate.
> With the long gabardine,
> with the yellow patch—burning—
> with proud stride
> I decide—:
> I am going back to the ghetto.
> Wipe out, stamp out all traces of apostasy.
> I wallow in your filth.
> Blessed, blessed, blessed,
> hunchbacked Jewish life.
> Go to hell, with your polluted cultures, world.
> Though all is ravaged,
> I am dust of your dust,
> sad Jewish life.
> . . .
> And though He tarries, I have hope;
> day in, day out, my expectation grows.
> Leaves will yet green
> on our withered tree.
> I don't need any solace.

I return to our cramped space.
From Wagner's pagan-music to chants of sacred humming.
I kiss you, tangled strands of Jewish life.
Within me weeps the joy of coming home.

Gedali, Gedali, some nights the heart catches!
It's out of tune. It hurts. It pounds. Paris is moving away, sinking
into the distance. Not even a memory. Memory dark with arms
laid down. No bottle in the ocean. Memory bleeds. Note all the
differences. All that would surely lend reality, all that would finally make her understand Quebec and Montreal and the language here, all that would end up taking on the configurations of
a new life. Especially, don't forget the list of St-Hubert Barbecue
restaurants in the yellow pages:

Restaurant	388 Dorval Ave. (Dorval) - - - - - - -
Delivery	10635 Pie IX Blvd.- - - - - - - - - - - -
Special price for take-out	4505 Jean-Talon E. - - - - - - - - - - -
Fully licensed	7979 Newman Blvd. (Lasalle) - - - -
Car orders	222 des Laurentides Blvd.
4462 St-Denis - - - - - - - - - - - - - - -	(Pont Viau) - - - - - - - - - - - - - - - -
6355 St-Hubert - - - - - - - - - - - - - -	3325 St-Martin Blvd. (Chomedey) -
862 Ste-Catherine E. - - - - - - - - - - -	111 St-Martin Blvd. (Laval) - - - - - -
4590 Ste-Catherine E. - - - - - - - - - -	1425 St-Charles E. (Longueuil) - - -
2152 Ste-Catherine W.- - - - - - - - - -	2315 Chambly (Longueuil)- - - - - - -
6225 Sherbrooke E. - - - - - - - - - - -	6325 Taschereau Blvd. (Brossard)
12575 Sherbrooke E. - - - - - - - - - -	4700 Montée St-Jean
684 Ste-Croix Blvd. (St-Laurent)- - -	(Pierrefonds)- - - - - - - - - - - - - - -

Mime Yente would do her shopping in Snowdon. Early Friday morning she would bustle around Steinberg's on Queen
Mary and pick up her meat across the street at Calvados and her
bread at her former bakery near Isabella. She'd know the neighbourhood by heart, having lived there since before the construction of the Décarie autoroute. She would never have wanted to
sell her lopsided duplex; she was too attached to the memory of
Moishe, the rose bushes in the garden, the neighbourhood.
"The samovar can't be moved," she would mutter between her

teeth when the question of her moving came up. "Not the samovar, not my rose bushes, not Bilou, and not me. Period."

Mime Yente. Mime Yente from Zhitomir, Zhitomir on the
Teterev. Sister, mother, or daughter of old Gedali of Volhynia,
you finally found your country in Snowdon, in the little area of
land bounded by Queen Mary and Côte-Ste-Catherine, and
Hampstead, Notre-Dame-de-Grace, and Victoria. You feel at
home there. A little like the *barbudo* at home in his "hole" on the
Main up near Jean Talon, in his little area between Jean-Talon
and Van Horne, Avenue du Parc and St-Vallier. Everyone here
in his or her little refuge-rectangle with its streets and points of
reference.

> Its bits of dreams—patched-together city,
> city of juxtaposed exiles,
> of piled-up solitudes that touch without seeing each
> other
> no invisible mending, all the seams show.
> Stray words
> > adrift
> > without anchors.
> Foreign words in incomprehensible idioms,
> words of lost communion
> > of broken connections
> words that meet blindly in the city,
> naked words
> other words,
> immigrant words.

MÉTRO OPÉRA. The nice neighbourhoods. Seamstresses
and shopgirls under the arcades of Rue Rivoli in the old days before Mitsubishi, electronics, the express lines of the métro, and le
drugstore. The days of things from Paris, silk scarves. Smile,
Mimi. An American in Paris. The old wound would open.
Hands off memories. The Opéra before Chagall's ceiling. It was

Verdi's *La Traviata*. Verdi is usually at the Opéra Comique, isn't it? No, it was definitely *La Traviata*. I had a big mauve bow in my hair, white socks, black patent leather sandals, and a dress with smocking. I was holding my breath. I didn't understand anything. They were singing in Italian but the lady looked as if she was suffering a lot and I liked the music. At intermission I stuffed myself with chocolate and Gervais ice cream. In those days, the nice salty Bahlsen crackers didn't exist, nor did pico-rettes, but there was Nestlé's chocolate and vanilla or praline Gervais ice cream. I had gone to the opera! So that was what that big building was that looked a little like a cake there in the middle when you came out of the métro. Around the Opéra métro station, in the little streets near the Comédie Française, there were still inexpensive bistrots where they served moules marinière with muscadet on bare wood tables. At the zinc counter, the owner recounted the story of his trials and tribulations and there were heavy sighs before the laughter. This was not the Paris of the bourgeois. No. Nothing to do with that ad in one of the latest issues of *Le Monde:* "Believe it or not, the height of luxury is more affordable than you'd think. It might seem impossible to put Paris at your feet in the heart of the 15th arrondissement for 12 500 to 18 000 F a square metre. And yet that's the price of the prestige apartments Totem is offering, from studios to 3 or 4 rooms. Totem, an ultra-luxurious building 200 metres from the Eiffel Tower. Contact us to visit this exceptional building.

Totem. Capri. 5750 Quai de Grenelle, 75015, Paris."

Grenelle. Yes, Grenelle. I don't know any more. The line gets lost in my memory. It was nice out that Thursday. Around Rue Nelaton, Rue Nocard, after Grenelle.

Her novel on the false messiahs of Jewish History, or rather on how her character Morton Himmelfarb would talk about them, would remain stuck for many weeks. Old Morton being re-luctant or discouraged, or too sick. Panicked, she would work twice as hard. Old Morton would be at his work table preparing his course, having decided this time to put the emphasis on the third reincarnation of the divine soul, Jacob Frank.

"In the beginning, in the beginning." Yes, begin at the beginning. But with false messiahs, once it begins, it doesn't stop. That's the tragedy. Interminable. Forty-five hours, fifteen classes to talk about Jacob Frank to know-nothings. No sense of History. No historical memory, don't know anything. How to go about it? Natasha, help me. To stay at my desk nice and warm and look out the window at the snowstorm assailing the naked maple tree, stay there nice and warm in my bathrobe with a good hot coffee, books all over the desk, files in a mess, pencils not sharpened. To stay there for hours looking for a way to present Jacob Frank. It isn't easy, I'll say as an introduction on the first day, if I don't have an asthma attack that day, but there will still always be a first class. It's hard to remember, with Jacob Frank, that it's the middle of the eighteenth century. If they want to be smart, they can always say that's true with orthodox rabbis too—and certain other people. A jab at me. But they're not smart alecks. Three hours of general background, the organization of the course, the bibliography, fourteen classes to go. An asthma attack, a strike, or a bad snowstorm—thirteen three-hour classes to go. He was born in Podolia, I'll say. Who knows where Podolia is? Silence in the class. Of course, they don't know anything. It's in the southwest Ukraine, between the Dniester and the Bug. Better provide a map here. Very early, Jacob Frank was in contact with the Sabbataians. Now, I'm not going to go back to Sabbatai Sevi. We already looked at that in another life, another chapter, and even if it didn't concern you, that's no reason. He began to read the Zohar. Who knows what the Zohar is? Silence. Three hours on the Zohar. Come on. "Woe to the sinners who take the Torah for mere fables about the things of this world, seeing only the outer garment. Happy are the just whose gaze penetrates to the Torah itself. As the wine must be put in a decanter in order to keep, so the Torah must be wrapped in an outer garment. This garment

consists of fables and stories. But we must penetrate beyond it."
And you too, try not to let yourselves be taken in by appearances,
by the garment, the fable, the story! To tell History or stories.
Tell the story of Jacob Frank's life. Pay attention, the exam will be
hard and you won't have your notes. Morton Himmelfarb gloats.
Morton sky-colour is already thinking of exam questions to trick
them with. Idiots, don't know anything.

These false messiahs all had the wanderlust and they were
all attracted to the Ottoman Empire. It's true that Jews were safer
there than in the Christianity of the Inquisition. So, Jacob travelled, I'll say. I'll tell the story. First he married Hannah, because
his master had said he would initiate him into the secrets of the
sect when he married. Then he travelled, I'll say, he went to Adri-
anople and to Smyrna, he meditated on the grave of Nathan of
Gaza, and then he went to Salonica. He returned to Podolia.
Show his route on the map. That little trip took twenty-five years.
Noise in the class. Digress to a lecture on "time in history." That
will take a good three hours. When he got back, he had a turban
on his head and his enemies said he took part in all kinds of or-
gies. Imprisoned, released, imprisoned, released. Went back to
Turkey and converted to Islam. A real epidemic, these false Messiahs who went over to Islam. Written test. Why did Sabbatai Sevi
and Jacob Frank convert? Silence in the class. You have three
hours. Natasha, don't look at me like that, I know this is not serious, but History, you know, isn't always serious. Old sky-colour
can't any more. He's sick. He dreams only of staying in his
study on Sunday morning in his bathrobe with his kimmel
bread, Philadelphia cream cheese and lox, and a good hot coffee, in the midst of his piles of books and file folders, watching
the wan sky, the snow, and the wind shaking the topmost
branches of the maple tree. Morton sky-colour no longer waits
for the Messiah. Just for calm, silence, rest.

Okay, so the masses began to agitate. Anyway, you can't go
wrong. In History books, either the masses don't exist or they're

apathetic or they swallow everything or they agitate. Here, they agitated. In Galicia, the Ukraine, Hungary, and Moravia. Poor Jacob was excommunicated in 1756 with all the members of his sect, the reading of the Zohar was practically forbidden (those rabbis didn't fool around), and then, just when Jacob was about to engage in complicated "disputations" with the rabbis, when the course is finally going to become theoretical, difficult, even scholarly, Morton Himmelfarb dies of a heart attack at his desk. Just like that. On a Sunday morning, one of those winter Sundays he loved so much, a Sunday of snow, a wan sky, dull light, and high winds. Just like that, without finishing his hot coffee and his slices of bread, just like that in the midst of his piles of books and file folders, without the help of Natasha, far, very far, from his native Vitebsk, alone. The course gone, all traces gone, the merry-go-round of false messiahs gone. We'll never know what became of Jacob Frank. The masses that had begun to agitate are waiting. To tell History or to tell stories. Morton sky-colour is dead.

> Don't lose your bearings. Here it's hard
> not to become the same
> not to fall into line.
> Careful.
> The viets are watching you,
> the nyets are looking,
> the popovs will attack you,
> the poor will come pillage you.
> Put up barricades!
> Arm yourself to the teeth!
> Even your neighbour can't be trusted!
> Pray to God. Things will get better.
> Nothing can be done. We're doing our best.

Look, my dear, they're saying in the salons where they sip champagne at boring vernissages, you don't realize. If the guerillas win in El Salvador, it will be the gulag. Poor things! Maybe the junta and Reagan are overdoing it a bit, but still, you don't realize!

Buy some gizmo
and pay in ten years.
Get everything.
If you can't pay, even on credit,
DROP DEAD.

You don't have to be Greek to love the restaurants and shops on Park Avenue.

Mime Yente, tired of seeing him skin his hands like that, would finally have gone to see old Morgenstern, who had a secondhand store on Parc between St-Viateur and St-Joseph. Old Morgenstern, whom she'd meet at the theatre, at Sunday brunch, or at the bagel factory, would have mentioned that he was thinking of calling it quits but wanted to turn the shop over to someone he could trust. One summer evening when they were saying goodbye to her among the rose bushes, she would have spoken to them about the secondhand store, old Morgenstern, and the apartment above the store, on the second floor. They would have been thrilled with the idea. They would already be building a thousand castles in the air. They would have gone without a murmur from Italy to Greece. *Morning Star Antiques: Étoile du Matin* in big childish yellow letters. He would have repainted the storefront apple green and scrubbed the windows clean. He would have put an old pine table out on the sidewalk with some brass, glass, and china pieces and some bells on it, and a pair of old purple high-backed chairs on either side of the door. So customers could sit down and have a chat and a pipe with him. Profit wouldn't be everything. There would be time. All they needed would be to pay old Morgenstern his rent and to live as best they could by selling odds and ends. Bilou would have taken a liking to the store, lolling on the chairs outside in the sun or under the pots of flowers hanging at the door. In one of the windows she would have put a mannequin from the twenties in a gorgeous dress of black paillettes, with some old irons and chipped Empire china, and in the other window a platform scale with its weights. Inside it would be dark, crammed with an amazing array of furniture that needed to be stripped, kerosene lamps, samovars of every kind, and brass pieces straight from the market in Athens or Heraklion. And potbellied bottles, gourds, cowbells, bed warmers, and curling irons. You could spend hours rummaging through the boxes piled willy-nilly on top of an old sewing machine, finding mother-of-pearl buttons, old coins, children's dolls from the turn of the century, single gloves. At the back of the store would be a bistrot table with an old-fashioned cash register on it and another rickety old high-backed chair. There old Morgenstern would have sat, his hat on his head in all seasons, waiting for hypothetical customers and reading old Hebrew manuscripts by the light of a kerosene lamp. Near him, a barrel organ that he would always have refused to sell because he enjoyed playing it, taking it out on the sidewalk on summer afternoons and attracting the kids from the neighbourhood. All the way in the back, a white rocking horse that hadn't rocked in a century and couldn't be repaired would have its glass eyes fixed on the disorder of this secondhand store on the skids.

They would have moved into a long, narrow apartment on the second floor, with thick walls, looking out on Avenue du Parc. All his Latin American and Italian friends would have come for the housewarming. He would quickly have become acquainted with the Greeks in the neighbourhood, almost instinctively able to identify those who had been in prison under the junta of the colonels and those who were a little older and had been in the Resistance and the civil war—on the right side, of course. Already they would be acquiring new habits, tracing new routes in this opaque city. Already they would have their new restaurants, restaurants that served seafood, souvlaki, yogurt with cucumber, accompanied by ear-splitting bouzouki music.

Already they would have identified the cafés where they could spend hours reading the newspapers. They'd just have to close the door on the secondhand store, leaving Bilou on one of the chairs and hanging the "back in a few minutes" sign on the apple green door. In this neighbourhood of southern peoples, nobody would mind. You could spend hours reading newspapers, preparing classes, reading poetry, and talking. Greece and the common market and the municipal elections in Athens and the tourists who were transforming the Plaka and the neighbourhoods of Heraklion beyond recognition. He would give his opinion on everything, his fingers in his pouch of shag tobacco. She would enjoy going to the bagel bakery on St-Viateur, which was open twenty-four hours a day. She would talk Yiddish with the owner, who would have taken her for a newly arrived Polish Jew and kept asking, "So, how are things in Lublin now? Do you know Chaim Gleys?"

She would look at him nonplussed, watching his hands working the dough. "Look, I was born in Paris, I've never been to Poland!"

"Oh, okay," he would say, skeptical, kneading the dough, "You've got an accent like someone from there."

To make amends, she would buy piles of bagels, white ones with sesame seeds and black ones with poppy seeds. What is it that gives this city its haunting charm? Its special smell? Spice city, fuchsia city, pumpkin seed city, pistachio city. They would have no answer, would let themselves sink into the summer sea of its obscure vapours, faint, overcome with well-being. Sometimes, no more longing. They would as time went by have more and more Québécois friends, all in agreement on one thing:

"When will this left come?"

"What about the left of the PQ, what's it doing?"

"And what about the CSN?"

"So let's get a move on, right?"

Quietly, without saying anything, without expressing it clearly to themselves, they would feel things changing around them. Quebec would be moving quietly, imperceptibly toward a plural society. Witnesses of this unconscious metamorphosis, they would also be its obscure, anonymous authors.

Morning Star Antiques Étoile du Matin. Bilou would have stayed with them, going back and forth between the old purple high-backed chairs and the piano on the second floor. Sometimes when there were five or six people in the shop, she would make tea in a samovar. And they would talk for a long time without anyone buying anything, which, incidentally, would worry Mime Yente a bit. They would also play card games or dice or do card tricks, at which a Greek restaurant owner was a master. One of the regulars in the shop would be Shloime Reisen, a funny character, a *luftmensch,* one of a kind. He would bum around for days with all his worldly possessions in a packsack: a few books, a change of underwear, a wash-and-wear shirt, a sweater, various keys that wouldn't open anything, and a few cans of tuna. He would "borrow" a car and disappear for days at a stretch, and then reappear fat or thin like his bag, which might be as flat as a pancake or as round as a ball. On his return, Shloime would have a mysterious air and no one would ask any questions. Another regular and hero would be Malcolm Burns. Malcolm had never had any luck. No skills, no trade, nothing. Hardly hired at a garage on Avenue du Parc, he would have been fired when the boss discovered he didn't know how to drive. Then he would have found work at a cemetery for a week or two, but as he liked to say, "It's not a life." So he would hang around the shop, playing cards and reading the past instead of the future in people's palms.

One day old Morgenstern, whom they would rarely have seen since his retirement to Côte-St-Luc, would have come by with a magic lantern he'd found on a trip to Prague. They would have turned off the lights in the store and operated it, and a succession of colourful figures would have moved across the wall, old-fashioned figures reminiscent of eighteenth century automatons or the drawings in children's schoolbooks from Weimar Germany.

Note all the differences. The plates on the front and back of the cars. Je me souviens. I love Montreal. I love my wife. The logo of the Canadiens or the Expos, or names of people or places: Gaspé, Rivière-du-Loup, St-Georges-de-Beauce. And once, an exception: Allende te recuerdo, Chile no te olvido. The Italian flag, the Greek flag, or the maple leaf or the *fleur de lys*, or the blue and red together, the maple leaf and the *fleur de lys*.

Note everything. Forget nothing. The urgency. Store everything, as if you were to find yourself like Robinson on his island and were to encounter Montreal only through traces, signs, symbols, meaningless fragments, pieces, debris, useless shards. The obsessive love of lists, inventories, archives. Historian of nothing, of the ephemeral. Anxiety of the trace to be kept. Never dust anything. Not houseclean, not breathe for fear that your own breath scatter these few remains. Keep everything. Store everything. Create all these memories in advance. Yellowed newspapers, cheques, income tax forms, old credit cards, grab-bag, odds and ends never organized, never emptied, thick strata of the dead everyday. Not houseclean. Keep all the traces. Create in your head or on paper your own Morning Star Antiques.

Gedali, who to write for?

and in what language?

The Hassidim of Outremont speak Yiddish, but what do I have in common with them aside from the work of words and memory?

Métro Grenelle. After Grenelle. I don't know any
more

The line gets lost in my memory
Jews
must

169

use

the

last

car.

It was nice out on July 16, 1942

around Rue Dr Finlay

Rue Nocard

Rue Nelaton.

Around Grenelle, the 15th arrondissement.

Wurden vergast.

The operation was called

SPRING WIND.

Never returned.

Around Grenelle.

Gedali, who remembers?

Immigrant words disturb. They don't know how to find the right pitch. Too high, they don't ring true. Too low, they're deranged. They slip out of control, go astray, go crazy, languish, repeat themselves shamelessly, nonplussed, puffed up, and anemic in turn. Immigrant words disrupt. They displace, transform, work the very fabric of this fragmented city. They have no place. They can only designate exile, elsewhere, outside. They have no inside. Words living and dead at the same time, full words. Immigrant words are unplaceable, untenable. They're never where you look for them, where you think they are. They don't move in. Words without territory or anchor, they've lost their colours and intonations. They can't be attached. Feta words, bagel words, pistachio words, pepper words, cinnamon words, they've lost their name, their language, their smells.

Gedali, who to write for and in what language? Morose morning star. Morton sky-colour, sad, wan. *Barbudo* lost in the back of your secondhand store, your pipe of shag tobacco in your mouth, Bilou on your purple chair, Mime Yente by your

170

samovar from Zhitomir, and you and I and she walking in this city, which is crumbling in you, which is disappearing in you.

It is true that the just man said, "You remember for all eternity all that is forgotten." No more will you walk in the snow in the evening after a storm, when the sky has cleared and brightly lighted interiors with logs burning in the fireplaces in the living rooms can be seen from the street. No more will you go in the spring and see the lilacs in the gardens of Notre-Dame-de-Grâce, no more will you go to the Marché Jean-Talon in summer to get tomatoes, braids of garlic, and peppers. No more will you stroll on Avenue du Parc in search of a Greek friend met long ago in Delphi chatting up the tourists. No more will you walk along St-Urbain or the Main and hear the rough language of Janos, Janos of Rose Hill and Margaret Island. No more will you see the rose bushes in the gardens of Westmount or Outremont or hear the cries of children in the east end. No more will you go to the stripped-wood bistrots of Rue St-Denis or Drolet. No more bagels from St-Viateur or smoked meat at Schwartz's, no more cheese-cake at Pumpernik's. No more will you spend hours listening to the silence broken by the sound of the planes beginning their descent into Dorval.

> Exhausted undoubtedly,
> Broken up.

One day, just like that, she would have decided to leave. Mime Yente would have shrugged her shoulders and made no attempt to stop her, nor would he at the back of the shop behind the bistrot table and the old cash register, nor Bilou lolling on one of the bright purple high-backed chairs. Nor anybody. She would have taken the plane from Mirabel, Air France, at 20:45. The books would follow by air freight and a few pieces of furniture by boat in a container. France would have changed.

She would take the métro again, just like that, out of habit, without ever going past Grenelle.

LA MOTTE PIQUET-GRENELLE. The Canon de Grenelle. Grey noisy metal of the elevated métro. The Bouquet de Grenelle. The Bar des Sports. Le Pierrot. Paris is disintegrating. No order—no chronology, no logic, no story. Nothing but Paris at the Grenelle métro.

Collections. Lists. Inventories. The magic of proper names. She would be back in the same bistrots.

"A decaf, please, and a pack of Gauloises, non-filter."

Once more the wet grey Paris of her adolescence, once more the racket of slot machines, the anonymous murmur in the back of bistrots, the squealing brakes at red lights, the green crosses of pharmacies reflected in puddles. Once more the demonstrations from La Nation to La République, the May 1st parades. Once more . . . by the way, it seems the Place du Québec is in Saint-Germain-des-Prés.

The Writing of an Allophone from France[1]

Afterword to *The Wanderer* Fifteen Years Later

Migrant writing, writing in exile, writing that cannot "set down" anywhere, that is never at rest. It seems to me that when I wrote this book it was a kind of therapy for me. In the first place, it allowed me to stay in Quebec. It was written just after the first referendum and published in 1983. I had the feeling that I had to say something about my relationship with this place, and I found the form in which to do so not in the essay but rather in the novel, in narrative. I needed the voice of a writer, not that of an academic. Through this experiment, I sought to find out what a French Jewish intellectual from Paris whose parents had immigrated to France from Poland a few years before the war could say about her being in exile. The reader will have noticed that "she," the character in the novel, always ends up leaving and going back to Paris.

The novel was greeted with some ambivalence. I think it was a revelation for many people. The reviews were quite favourable and it was praised for its form and writing. There was also an increasing number of scholarly essays and articles, especially after the book's second edition ten years later in a small-format paperback, in the vein of "as soon as she talks about Paris, she waxes lyrical and has a tremor in her voice, but when she talks about *us* in Quebec, there's always something she doesn't like." In other words, I was accused of not understanding Quebec, of

---

1. Translator's note: In the special vocabulary used to describe the linguistic reality in Quebec, an *allophone* is a person whose first language is neither French nor English.

not liking Quebec, of seeing only the negative, keeping myself at a distance, marginalizing myself. There was a whole little "psychodrama" around The Wanderer—which did not displease me at all.

Writing this book was vital and valuable for me. Had I not begun to write it, I would have gone back to Paris as my character did. I wrote it because it allowed me to explore a problem that I was unable to express in other ways. One leitmotif in the book is that one does not become Québécois. After writing the book I understood that becoming Québécois was no longer of any importance to me. *The Wanderer* deals with the problem of finding a place for oneself here and making one's voice heard when one comes from elsewhere, and once the book was finished, I felt that this was possible through writing, through social involvement, through the practice of one's craft, through friendship and other relationships—and so I turned a page.

At the beginning, I found myself in all kinds of curious situations. To me, PC could only mean the Communist Party or a personal computer, never a political party that called itself "progressive conservative," which is an oxymoron. This used to make me laugh until I cried. And I remember a newspaper headline from shortly after I arrived in Quebec: "Red sweep in Quebec." I cut it out and sent it, without the story, to my friends in Paris. They rushed to their television sets and radios to find out if there had been a revolution here. But no, it was only an election victory by the Liberal Party. In Europe at that time, those words had a very different meaning!

I am basically a city person, a daughter of the world's great capitals, a person who, when in good health, was a night owl and spent my time in bistrots or walking the streets, making the city mine. My character and/or I appropriates the city by walking in it, observing it. All the lists in *The Wanderer* are my way of becoming familiar with the new place and assimilating it. They also involve memory; while I am becoming familiar with Montreal, I am creating a memory of this new place. From the start of *The*

Wanderer, I was aware that things would very quickly become ordinary to me, that I would no longer see them with the same eyes, that I would be "tamed" by this new city. When you're in a new place, the first thing that disappears is the strangeness; you become accustomed. I had to act while everything was still strange. I wanted to make note of everything before it became mine, to capture the feeling of strangeness.

MIGRANT WRITER OR NEO-QUÉBÉCOIS WRITER?

There is a paradox in the Quebec literary establishment. On one hand, Quebec massively rejects the Canadian policy of multiculturalism. On the other hand, assimilation in the French manner (integration of individuals rather than communities) is not possible in North America. We therefore find Quebec promoting "interculturalism," which often (not always) brings together the best and the worst of the French and the American systems. Quebec literature is not a "hyphenated" literature such as those found in societies that are increasingly structured along ethnic lines. A new term has been created to designate writing by immigrant novelists, poets, or playwrights: neo-Québécois literature. This literature is not relegated to the margins of the literary establishment, but the designation neo-Québécois is a way of marking immigrant writers, and it indicates that there is a problem.

Many of Quebec's writers fall into this category. They are of very diverse origins and come from every part of the world, and their æsthetic concerns are equally varied. What they have in common, beyond this designation as neo-Québécois writers, is being immigrants to Quebec—and for some of them, being in exile—writing in French, whether it is their mother tongue, a second language, or a recent acquisition, finding themselves in the midst of the endless political tension around identity in Quebec, and expressing in their writing another tension—between the memories, language or languages, smells, sights, and culture of their country of origin and those of their host country, in North

America but with its own distinct language and culture and its sometimes undecodable explorations of its identity. This work in the in-between, inside-outside, between-languages, this wandering, this gaze of someone from elsewhere characterizes the migrant literature that plays such an important role in the examination of new identities. Neo-Québécois writers have been forcing open the doors of the literary establishment in their striving to renew the forms of writing, narrative structures, existential questions, and the social imaginary of Quebec. This hybrid writing, which is profoundly North American, Québécois, and francophone— and eminently cross-cultural—belongs to the postmodern evolution of societies that today, more than ever, are destined to be culturally plural.

It may well be that all this is only a transitory situation, and that one day the "neo-Québécois" writers and the "old-stock" writers may exist together with no distinctions as to their origins. Simply writers, simply writing. After all, isn't Quebec's greatest poet of exile Jacques Brault? One catches oneself dreaming of the transcendence of boundaries and labels.

But that dream is still very far from reality. In a recent publication, writer and critic Monique LaRue presents a hypothetical colleague who is filled with resentment of the success of a new generation of immigrant writers whose works

> have nothing to do with what we have always called Quebec literature, have no relation to the history of Quebec or the logic of its development, do not pursue its search for identity or draw on its stock of references, its intertextual relationships, its imaginary, and do not integrate into their culture any of the linguistic or stylistic features that characterize Quebec literature . . . and yet these writers are allowed to represent Quebec literature to the world at international conferences.[2]

---

2. *L'Arpenteur et le Navigateur* (Montreal: Fidès and Cétuq, 1996), p. 8. Translator's note: my translation.

LaRue lambastes this position, which she calls the *"Pravda syndrome,"* recalling that publication's refusal to recognize Nobel laureate Joseph Brodsky as a Russian poet because he did not sing the praises of Russia or the Russian people. For the hack who wrote his obituary in *Pravda,* Brodsky was a Jewish poet who at best could be said to write in Russian.

There is no point wondering if LaRue's envious writer is "real" or if she has created him as a personification of the demons that continue to haunt Quebec writers, even those with the best of intentions. LaRue voices questions of her own:

> Up to now our literature has been the expression of a relatively homogeneous shared world and common experience, and we have not asked ourselves what a Québécois writer is. If we are now able to think politically in terms of a heterogeneous, plural, diverse, and cosmopolitan Quebec, then on the literary level, what will the literature of this Quebec be? Will we still be able to speak of a national literature? How do we think about the fusion of Quebec literature as it has existed up to now with literature as others see it? . . . With such a diversity of perspectives, will it still be possible to speak of "a" literature . . . or will there be as many literatures as there are ethnic groups? (p. 11)

A few years ago I took part in an evening with migrant writers of many nationalities. The question being discussed, which was an unusual but enlightening one, was: what is your literary nationality? There is nothing less obvious than the answer to this seemingly oxymoronic question. The easiest answers may be in terms of where your publishers are, whom you sign publishing contracts with, and of course, what language you write in. These answers provide some important initial truths. But for some writers, even on this level nothing is simple, because one can write in two languages or work in two literary fields, or write only in one language but be attached to two different institutions.

Identity as lived by the writer is another matter. To what nationality should a writer pay literary allegiance? Is one a French writer? A Québécois writer? A French-speaking Canadian writer? A Jewish writer? A French-Jewish writer? A Québécois Jewish writer? A Canadian Jewish writer? An allophone Jewish writer of French origin? A Montreal writer? You could go on forever. Unless one has a very strong fixation on a definition of identity, things are very complicated.

None of this says anything about another level that needs to be considered with writers, and that is how identity works within their writing, how the back-and-forth movements of identity are inscribed in their texts. Who is the implied reader for whom they are writing? That is where the semblance of an answer to the question would be found. Who can understand the text, who has the implicit knowledge to decode the cultural messages of the text? Of course, we are not imprisoned in our own culture and memory, or translation would be impossible. I do not have to know the Russian landed gentry or the czar's army in order to appreciate *Anna Karenina,* for example. The implied reader in *The Wanderer,* the one from whom I unconsciously demand immediate understanding, who can share even my most tenuous allusions—a date, the name of a street, a song, a café—would initially be a certain type of French person. But then I refer to Jewish history and Sabbatai Sevi, the false messiah, and my implied reader changes to become a Jew. And then at another point, the discussion of issues in Quebec comes to the forefront, and there my implied reader is a Quebecker.

Literature is often a debate with one's multiple identities. That is why the question of literary nationality cannot be answered. There are no literary passports or visas. As might have been guessed, for me there is no "innocent" nationalism—neither of the small, lowly, and obscure, nor of the great, the threatening, those that have truly shown their colours—any more than there can be innocent domination, even when it is masked by the smiles of the jolly characters of Disneyland. Literature is a specific place for the play of imagination, experimentation, and questioning of one's own identity/ies. While the subject of women —even a woman's voice—or ethnic or minority status may be inscribed in writing, literature is the place where all ties of belonging and identity are problematized. What does it mean to be a woman in a literary text? How can the feminine be defined in literature? What does it mean to be "ethnic"? We have to go beyond binary models and look at what weakens the ideology of mastery, whether it be in terms of identity or of language. The same is true for ethnicity. All identity—minority or not—too tightly defined, is a ghetto. Only literary works today allow the exercise of the full power of fantasy.

On the evening I referred to, I defined myself as "an allophone from France," which was of course greeted with laughter. To me, blasphemy and sacrilege, or simply irony, parody, and distancing, are part of a much-needed diversion of cultures. There are many of us who are trying to write in one language while dreaming of a second one that is barred to them. Should we try to forget that lost, pariah language? Freud invented a universal language, and Kafka, in his own unique German, altered legends and made the language fragile. Elias Canetti rediscovered his grandfather's orality in the market of Marrakech, and Georges Perec used palindromes to simulate writing simultaneously in French (left to right) and Yiddish or Hebrew (right to left).

In search of a new meaning in the past, I use false biography, false autobiography: "autofiction," the novel in the true sense. Autobiographical elements are inscribed in the narrative and transformed into fiction. Thus *The Wanderer* is not autobiographical in the customary sense. For example, the logic of the novel requires that my character not know how she would have voted in the first referendum, that all possibilities be left open. (In any case, she, like the author, would not have had the right to vote at that time.) I, Régine Robin, would have voted no in 1980, as I did in 1995. My character is fictional, nothing more than a narrative prop. I move her into three neighbourhoods of Montreal and give her Ukrainian origins, an aunt who emigrated from the Ukraine to Montreal by way of London, and a New York friend who may or may not resemble my husband. All these details are invented. While the novel does contain autobiographical elements, they are not necessarily attached to the main character but are disseminated throughout. Some are given to the writer who is trying to write a novel about Sabbatai Sevi, others to characters "she" encounters. So if *The Wanderer* is autobiography, it is intellectual or spiritual, not factual, autobiography.

Let me add that I find this book as fresh as if it had been written last year. Although Steinberg stores have been replaced by Métro and the prices of houses that once seemed staggering now appear paltry, not much has changed in the area of intercultural relations and the situation of the famous "ethnics." But there is one thing that has changed for me personally, and that is that I have gradually learned English, which—having been educated in France, where it has never been taught seriously—I understood and spoke badly. Paradoxically, what Quebec has given me is English. I now count it among "my" languages, and I am delighted. While this may not be a traditional position, it is that of a writer who, while writing in only one language (I am as attached to French as the hermit crab is to its shell), is inhabited by others—in dialogue, in symbiosis, in conflict.

It appears that the cross-cultural is now no longer in fashion—although for some of us, it was never just a fashion. These are bad times, especially for writers: fear of globalization, retreat back to "national" values, anxiety about the dissolution of identities. Another Quebec critic, Serge Cantin, personifies this trend. According to him, "Leonard Cohen . . . born and raised in a Montreal Jewish family, is not and never will be a Québécois *chansonnier*," because not only does he not write in French, but he also, "like so many other Montreal anglophones, is not, and has never aimed to become, Québécois—or rather, he is not Québécois because he has never aimed to become Québécois."[3] Cantin takes issue with the view of Quebec society as made up of a variety of ethnic groups, with francophones constituting the majority group. For him, the adoption of the name Québécois in the early sixties by those who had called themselves French Canadians, and before that simply *Canadiens,* was and still is a symbol of self-affirmation and political awakening in the face of the domination of the French nation of North America. There is little place in his definition for any other ethnic groups.

I write novels and short stories and non-fiction in French. But in Cantin's eyes, I cannot be a Québécois writer any more than Richler or Cohen. Not that I'm sure I'd want to be one in his eyes. I am, I repeat, an allophone from France. These are bad times indeed for the "others," the "neos," etc.

A few years ago at a conference in Argentina, I imagined that all writers were imprisoned in a kind of "soft" concentration camp somewhere in Patagonia, in the middle of nowhere, where they could continue to write and even publish within prescribed limits. They kept on writing—except for a few who couldn't accept the situation and fell into a state of depression, and a few others who committed suicide right after their incarceration—they kept on writing and arguing among themselves. But what was most interesting was what went on outside the camp. The world continued to turn as before with its wars and its concerns, and absolutely no one noticed that there were no more writers, no more writing, no more fantasies (thanks to technology, they could all be realized), no more creative imagination, no more dreams (what need would there be for the family romance if you could program the children and even the parents you wanted?).

---

3. *Ce pays comme un enfant* (Montreal: L'Hexagone, 1997), p. 85.
   Translator's note: my translation.

The absence of the writers went completely unnoticed in this age of prime-time television.

Is the writer, the "neo," above the fray, then? Not exactly. The writer is neither fully within nor fully outside. This is the position *The Wanderer* speaks from, watchful for the possibility of a rebirth of critical thought from the ashes, listening, waiting for something other, some new imaginary capable of expressing the diasporic evolution of the world.

April 1997

Notes

Pages 19–20: *The cemetery of a little Jewish town.* Isaac Babel, "The Cemetery at Kozin," *The Collected Stories,* ed. and trans. Walter Morison (New York: Meridian, 1960), p. 107.

Page 22: *A small and humble people* Adapted from Paul-Émile Borduas, "Refus global," *Total Refusal,* trans. Ray Ellenwood (Toronto: Exile, 1985), p. 27.

Page 27: *My town sad and gay!* Marc Chagall, *My Life,* trans. Elisabeth Abbott (New York: Orion, 1960), pp. 2, 94–95.

Page 28: *The foolish Jews* Quoted in Gershom Scholem, *Sabbatai Sevi: The Mystical Messiah* (Princeton: Princeton UP, 1973), p. 594. The quotations are from Abraham Abulafia.

Pages 29–30: *The modern reader* Gershom G. Scholem, *Major Trends in Jewish Mysticism* (New York: Schocken, 1961), pp.135–36.

Page 33: *An apparition* Gustav Meyrink, *The Golem,* trans. M. Pemberton (London: Dedalus, 1985), p. 59.

Page 51: *"A Pole closed my eyes,"* Adapted from Isaac Babel, "Gedali," *The Collected Stories,* ed. and trans. Walter Morison (New York: Meridian, 1960), pp. 70–72.

Pages 81–82: *On Russian fields* David Hofstein, "Poem," trans. Allen Mandelbaum, *A Treasury of Yiddish Poetry,* ed. Irving Howe and Eliezer Greenberg (New York: Holt Rinehart and Winston: 1969), pp. 173–74.

Page 111: *You are a dark amulet* M. Kulbak, "Vilna," trans. Nathan Halper, *A Treasury of Yiddish Poetry,* ed. Irving Howe and Eliezer Greenberg (New York: Holt Rinehart and Winston: 1969), pp. 218–19.

Page 128: *"I am ailing, Mademoiselle.* M. Kulbak, "Childe Harold," trans. Nathan Halper, *A Treasury of Yiddish Poetry,* ed. Irving Howe and Eliezer Greenberg (New York: Holt Rinehart and Winston: 1969), p. 211.

Pages 152–153: *My grandfather in Kobilnik* Moshe Kulback [sic], "My Grandfather," *An Anthology of Modern Yiddish Literature,* ed. Joseph Leftwich (The Hague: Mouton, 1974), pp. 276–77.

Pages 158–159: *Good night, wide world* Yankev Glatshteyn, "Good Night, World," *Selected Poems of Yankev Glatshteyn,* trans. and ed. Richard J. Fein (Philadelphia: Jewish Publication Society, 1987), pp. 101–3.

Régine Robin

Régine Robin was born in Paris of Jewish parents who left Poland to settle in France before World War II. Educated in France, she came to Quebec in the seventies and taught in several English and French universities. She has been at the Université du Québec à Montréal since 1982.

In addition to *The Wanderer (La Québécoite)*, Robin has written another novel, *Le Cheval blanc de Lénine* (1979), and a collection of stories, *L'immense fatigue des pierres* (1996). She has also published French translations of Yiddish writers and studies of Kafka, Yiddish, and socialist realism. *Le Réalisme socialiste, une esthétique impossible (Socialist Realism: An Impossible Aesthetic)* won the 1987 Governor General's Award for Non-fiction.

Régine Robin has been hailed as a major voice in a new Quebec literature of hybridity and exile. *Le Devoir* called her "Montreal's grande dame of postmodernism" for her groundbreaking work in literary theory. But she confesses that her true love is writing fiction. *The Wanderer* is the first of her fiction to be published in translation.

Phyllis Aronoff, translator

Phyllis Aronoff is a Montreal translator and editor. She has translated writings in philosophy, literary theory, science fiction, and theatre criticism, in addition to more mundane material. *The Wanderer* is her first book-length translation.